"You plan to wa̲̅ ̲̅ ̲̅ ̲̅ ̲̅ ̲̅ ̲̅ ̲̅ ̲̅ ̲̅ **on a date? I shou̲̅** ̲̅ ̲̅ ̲̅ ̲̅ ̲̅ **threatened, heart pounding because she couldn't believe he was even saying such nonsense.**

No way would he wait for her. Not that she wanted him to. She'd not really had a plan on when she'd start dating, or even if she would, just that she wouldn't while in school to avoid anything that might pull her away from success.

"Good, because I intend to hold you to our graduation day date. I know I did a train wreck of a job when I asked you to this party, so let me get this one right." He gave her one of his lopsided smiles. "Julia, will you give me the honor of taking you to dinner to celebrate earning your Master of Science in Nursing degree in May?"

Why did his question feel like so much more? As if her entire life depended upon her answer?

Dear Reader,

Nurse Julia Simmons is one of the most complicated heroines I've written. She is working hard to overcome past mistakes. To do that, she has life rules to keep herself on track to becoming the person she wants to be. Unfortunately, the hospital's new pulmonologist, Dr. Boone Riddle, tempts her to toss aside the rules she lives by. She won't give in, which means he'll have to wait. She doesn't believe he will, and if he does, her heart's in trouble because she's already on the verge of falling.

Boone doesn't understand why Julia insists on their being just friends until after she completes her master's in nursing program. If waiting six months for their first date is what he has to do, then so be it. She's worth waiting for. But when he discovers her past is similar to one that has already cost him someone he loved, dare he risk such loss again? Or has his heart already decided for him?

I hope you enjoy their story. If you'd like, feel free to reach out to me at janicemarielynn@gmail.com. Take care and much love.

Janice

BREAKING THE NURSE'S NO-DATING RULE

JANICE LYNN

HARLEQUIN

MEDICAL
ROMANCE

Recycling programs for this product may not exist in your area.

ISBN-13: 978-1-335-59522-5

Breaking the Nurse's No-Dating Rule

Harlequin Enterprises ULC
22 Adelaide St. West, 41st Floor
Toronto, Ontario M5H 4E3, Canada
www.Harlequin.com

Printed in U.S.A.

USA TODAY and *Wall Street Journal* bestselling author **Janice Lynn** has a master's in nursing from Vanderbilt University and works as a nurse practitioner in a family practice. She lives in the southern United States with her Prince Charming, their children, their Maltese named Halo and a lot of unnamed dust bunnies that have moved in after she started her writing career. Readers can visit Janice via her website at janicelynn.net.

Books by Janice Lynn

Harlequin Medical Romance

A Surgeon to Heal Her Heart
Heart Surgeon to Single Dad
Friend, Fling, Forever?
A Nurse to Tame the ER Doc
The Nurse's One Night to Forever
Weekend Fling with the Surgeon
Reunited with the Heart Surgeon
The Single Mom He Can't Resist
Heart Doctor's Summer Reunion

Visit the Author Profile page
at Harlequin.com for more titles.

**Janice won the National Readers' Choice Award
for her first book,
The Doctor's Pregnancy Bombshell.**

To those who don't allow past mistakes to
forever define who they are

CHAPTER ONE

"How do you stay so cheerful all the time? I've never seen you without a smile on your face. That can't be easy when you're surrounded by seriously injured and ill patients."

Intensive care nurse Julia Simmons smiled at her seventy-year-old patient's husband and wondered what the man would say if she told him the truth, that she strove to be a bright light in the hope that the darkness lurking deep within her never found its way out again. Yeah, that was way too heavy for an early Monday morning.

"I doubt anyone is cheerful all the time, but I do my best to choose happiness each day." She even had *Choose to be happy* listed in her Rules for Life Success notebook. Glancing toward the man's unconscious wife, her heart gave a painful squeeze. Irene Burch's viral pneumonia had sent her into respiratory failure, and she'd nearly died. Requiring life support to oxygenate her body, she seemed improved, but still might die. Working in the ICU meant knowing your patients were more likely to pass away than survive, but Julia did everything she could to increase their odds. "Some days are easier than others."

Taking a deep breath, the man nodded. "I know you're right. The past few days haven't been easy, but we've much to be thankful for. Irene is still with me and is improved some from when she was admitted earlier this week. Will Dr. Richards be by this morning to check on her?"

Cheeks hot, Julia averted her gaze at the mention of the hospital's newest pulmonologist. Had she thought Mr. Burch was going to see something in her eyes that she didn't want seen? That choosing happiness was all too easy when Dr. Boone Richards made his hospital rounds?

"Dr. Richards usually stops by the ICU prior to going to his office and then again after he finishes with his last appointment of the day." And sometimes in between when a patient had an issue. Not that she kept tabs.

Ugh. There went her cheeks bursting into flames again.

She finished checking her patient, assured Mr. Burch that she'd be close if anything changed, and stepped out of her patient's room. The moment she did, she scanned Knoxville General's intensive care unit. Boone was nearby. Exactly how she knew didn't make logical sense, but her awareness of when he was near happened too frequently to be coincidence. She figured it went back to some innate survival skill of sensing imminent danger. Despite how giddy being near him made her, she wasn't oblivious to the perils of getting too close.

Six feet tall, athletically built, quick-witted, and with the most appealing grin she'd ever seen, Boone was D-A-N-G-E-R. Not that she had a chance with him even if she did date—which she didn't. Boone was gorgeous and successful and the kind of guy that women like her admired from afar, but knew they didn't have a chance with in the real world. Plus, there was the beautiful orthopedic surgeon he had been dating since long before they'd came to Knoxville. She'd heard rumors they weren't together anymore, but she'd learned long ago not to pay much heed to gossip.

Spotting him, she bit her lower lip, watching him laugh at something a coworker said at the nurse station. Heavens, from the top of his shiny brown locks to the tips of his tennis shoes, he looked as if he starred on a television show rather than working as the highly skilled physician she knew him to be. Yeah, girls with pasts like hers didn't date men like Boone Richards, but even if they did, Julia had other plans for her life. No doubt he and the orthopedic surgeon made the perfect power couple and dazzled everyone who saw them together—if they were still a couple.

Boone's gaze shifted, pinning her with baby blues that had featured in more fantasies than she cared to admit. Immediately, he grinned, and a lot of thumps and bumps clanged around in her chest. Excusing himself from chatting with a respiratory therapist, he came to where Julia lingered at the hand sanitizer dispenser outside Mrs. Burch's room.

"Good morning, Julia. How's our lady holding up today?"

Despite how her blood raced through her vessels and made her a little light-headed, she met his gaze. "Becky was on shift last night. She reported that Irene remained stable. I cleared her airways with a suction catheter a few minutes ago and was pleased with her vitals. I believe she's improved some this morning."

"Great. I know you've just been in there, but will you round with me while I examine her?"

"Of course." It wasn't as if she'd refuse that request from any of the physicians she worked with, but Julia had major respect for Boone and enjoyed patient care with him. He was a great doctor. The best. She loved observing him with his patients and their families. Someday when she'd earned her master's and worked as a nurse practitioner, she imagined that she'd use him as a role model for the type of care she wanted to provide—professional, kind, and truly concerned for others.

"See, I said I'd be back soon," she told Mr. Burch when she reentered the ICU bay. "Look who I brought with me."

"Dr. Richards," the man greeted Boone, reaching out to shake his hand. Boone did so, then disinfected his hands prior to examining Irene.

After he'd checked her and answered her husband's questions the best he could, he dictated a few chart notes via his phone, then turned to Julia. "As you heard, I agree with you that Irene has improved some this morning. I'm decreasing her sedation in the hope that we can get her awake and wean her off the ventilator. Respiratory therapy should be by later this morning, and we'll start decreasing her ventilation settings."

Assessing the rise and fall of her patient's chest created by the lifesaving machine, Julia nodded. "I'll check regularly and keep you posted."

"Thanks."

"Use the call button if you need anything," she reminded Mr. Burch, then followed Boone from the room.

Rather than head toward the nurse station, he paused, chatting with her a few moments as they often did to discuss their favorites on a singing competition reality show they both enjoyed. Julia usually multitasked while exercising or house-cleaning, but she made a point to keep up with the show just so they could argue the merits of their favorites.

"The young girl from Kentucky whose father was a coal miner is going to win the whole thing," she assured him despite his claim that a male contestant would take final prize.

"So you keep telling me." One side of his mouth hiked up. Then he asked, "Are you going to the hospital Christmas party in a few weeks? I hear the hospital does a really great job putting the event together."

"They really do," she agreed. "Unless I'm needed here, I plan to go."

From the end of the fall term to the start of the spring semester, Julia got to breathe a little while not having classes, studying, and homework.

"That's great." His smile suggested it really was. "Are you bringing a plus-one?"

"No. At last year's, I was the plus-one for Stephanie and her boyfriend Derek." She laughed at the memory. Her bestie and coworker had insisted Julia join them as their designated driver and had made sure Julia didn't felt like a third wheel.

Boone's eyes sparkled like sunshine hitting the bluest sea. "Do you want to?"

Hello! She'd thought he was just chitchatting… Was he asking what she thought he was asking? Surely not. There was that whole out-of-her-league thing and the orthopedic surgeon he might or might not still be dating. Her heart pounded so hard it beat the air from her lungs, and she fought to keep from steadying herself by holding on to the wall. Did Boone want her to be his date, or was he trying to set her up with a friend? Or to just go with her as friends? In any case, no matter how insanely her heart raced, she shook her head.

"No plus-one for me. I don't date."

The sparkle in his eyes dimmed a little. "You don't date? As in, at all?"

She shrugged.

"Any particular reason why you don't date?"

She had dated once upon a time without thought or apparent care if the guy was a total loser—and she'd been with some doozies. After she'd straightened up her life, she'd bent her Rules for Life Success and dated a man she'd thought truly cared for her, even exposing her most shameful secrets to him. Of course, he'd never looked at her the same, teaching her a valuable lesson.

Wisely, she'd vowed to never stray again from the rules that had worked well for her thus far. Who had the time or energy to date, anyway?

She had other life priorities that didn't include squandering precious time on relationships that never lasted. Just look at how Clay had left her despite his promises to love her forever.

Then there were her mother's many relationships prior to her passing. Her father wasn't any better. His most recent wedding had been his number four, and the last Julia had heard, they weren't living together. Yeah, dating didn't fit into her life plan. Maybe after she graduated from school in May, but not until after she'd checked that off her list.

"My reasons are really not any of your business, Dr. Richards." Perhaps it was thoughts of Clay that had raised her hackles and put the haughtiness in her voice.

Boone studied her a moment, probably wondering why she'd gone so tense. But rather than questioning her further, he brandished one of those smiles that made her think it might be okay to toss aside her rules and just bask in his attention for however long it lasted. The man was seriously more tempting than the tastiest chocolate when she was on a diet. Good thing she'd just been thinking of Clay, so she had a fresh reminder of the devastating blows delivered by caring for someone who couldn't love you back.

"Fair enough," Boone conceded. "But if you

change your mind about dating, I'm free the night of the Christmas party."

He was asking for himself.

Not that it mattered, but the idea he was asking for himself rather than someone else seemed surreal. Surely he meant as just friends?

"You're free that night so you want me to change my mind about dating and then ask you to be my date?"

He pretended to consider, then gave another lopsided grin. "Not exactly what I meant, but that works. I promise not to play hard to get."

Still shocked that he wanted to go to the Christmas party with her, even as friends, Julia dug deep for the fortitude to look him straight in the eye. "I wouldn't hold my breath if I were you."

"I don't have to hold my breath to feel breathless around you, Julia."

His admission stunned her, and her head spun. Self-preservation kicked in, and panic filled her. What was Boone doing? She needed to keep her eyes on the prize. The prize was not a date with the hospital's most gorgeous doctor. She'd secretly crushed on him but had never dreamed he'd share her interest. Well, she had dreamed, but that's all it had been. A silly, secret fantasy. "Don't you have a girlfriend?"

He shook his head. "Surely you know that we

wouldn't be having this conversation if I had a girlfriend. I'm single."

The rumors had been true. He and the orthopedic surgeon were no longer a couple.

"Good for you." She fought to cover her astonishment that he was interested in a date with her. Not that she hadn't caught him watching her more than once. She had. She'd figured it was because he'd noticed the way her brain turned to mush when he was near.

She was flattered, stunned, but she wouldn't waver. She had rules that were working for her, and she was sticking to them. She recalled much too well that ignoring her own rules had led to having her heart broken. She enjoyed her work relationship with Boone, and even her private fantasies, but that's all they could ever be.

She needed distance from him, physical and emotional. "If you'll excuse me, Dr. Richards, I'm going to log my new notes on Mrs. Burch. Have a good day."

He didn't follow her to the nurse station, but she felt his gaze boring into her with each step she took. She ordered her feet to keep moving one step in front of the other—*Don't fall...don't break into a run*—partially because she didn't trust them to move away from Boone rather than toward him. He'd just asked her to go to the hospital Christmas party *with him*.

He'd said she took away his breath. Oh, heavens. Her insides were shaking at his dreamlike comment. Did he feel how attracted she was to him and assume she'd be an easy distraction while he was in between girlfriends? She didn't want to think poorly of him, but maybe it would be better if she did. Anything to put up a wall between them.

"Your cheeks are red," Stephanie pointed out when Julia reached the nurse station. "Wouldn't have anything to do with our favorite hunky doctor you were just talking to and who is still looking your way, would it?"

"No." She fought the urge to glance toward Boone.

"Yeah, I don't believe you." Stephanie laughed, then asked, "What were you talking about that's got you so red-faced? It's rare I see you flustered."

"Our patient."

"Mrs. Burch is what's got you all twitterpated?" Stephanie eyed her suspiciously. "Is everything okay?"

"She's stable, and I'm not whatever that word is."

"Girl, you are so off-kilter. I'd give my right eye to have been a fly on the wall and hear what Dr. Richards said to you. There's that rumor going around that he and Dr. Cunningham are no longer an item."

"You know better than to believe rumors." Julia shrugged as if she couldn't care less. She shouldn't. Whether Boone was available did not matter. Julia wasn't available. She'd keep it to herself that Boone had mentioned going to the Christmas party. She knew what Stephanie would tell her to do. Her friend thought she worked too much and needed to let loose, that it was long past time for her to be over the past and Clay. There were some things her friend couldn't fully understand. Julia knew, though. Letting loose was why she now had to buckle down so strictly.

"Most of the time I'd agree with that." Stephanie propped her elbows on the desk. "But on this occasion, I'm inclined to think it's true. Too bad if not, because I was hoping that you two had finally admitted what everyone already knows."

Rubbing her finger over the small tattoo on her left wrist, Julia gulped. "What's that?"

Stephanie wagged her perfectly sculpted brows. "That the air sizzles when you two are in the same room."

Others could feel it? Her cheeks burned, but glancing toward Stephanie, she snorted as if her friend was way off base. "That's your own man-crazy, happy-in-love-so-everyone-else-must-be-too, fried brain you're hearing sizzling. I wish you the best. Derek is a great guy. However, in my experience, relationships don't last."

"Derek's and mine will last." Stephanie informed her with full-on sass. "But you keep telling yourself every guy is like Clay so that you can hide behind those walls you erected when he left. They aren't. Dr. Richards is a great guy. If he's single, you should invite him to dinner or something." She stuck her finger up in the air. "Sizzle. Sizzle."

Sizzling air around Boone or not, she wouldn't admit to there being anything more than professional admiration in the way she felt about Boone. Not to her friend. Nothing good could come from doing so. She was happy, healthy, and on course. The last thing she needed was a refresher course in Heartbreak 101.

Later that week, Dr. Boone Richards smiled at the petite brunette wearing a bright pink scrub top with colorful dancing cats on it. He was starting to blame her more and more for his discontent in life. Which wasn't fair to Julia. He had a great life, the career he'd always wanted, and he could have moved on to the next step in his personal life with Olivia. Instead, a few weeks back, he'd ended the five-year relationship that had led him to Knoxville. Olivia hadn't taken the breakup well. She'd been expecting an engagement ring, not a goodbye.

The reality was they should have ended it years ago but had grown so comfortable in their seemingly "perfect" life that they'd overlooked a really big thing they were missing. They weren't in love. No matter how much he'd tried, he'd been unable to picture himself growing old with her. As soon as he'd admitted that truth to himself, he'd set her free. Set them both free.

After that, things that should have been obvious all along gained clarity. Things like Julia Simmons and how much he looked forward to seeing her when he consulted in the intensive care unit. How he hoped she'd be the nurse taking care of his patients, so he'd have reason to directly interact with her because he enjoyed their chats and her cheerful enthusiasm in all she did.

Not that there had been enjoyable chats or cheerful enthusiasm that week. He'd ruined everything because she'd not met his gaze since his Christmas party invite, instead quickly disappearing whenever he came to the unit. Her avoidance was driving him crazy, but he could only blame himself. He hadn't asked a woman on a first date in five years and had majorly botched his attempt.

"Dr. Richards." She averted her gaze, staring at the med cart drawer she'd just closed. "Mrs.

Burch has done well with the decreased pressures on her ventilator. Do you intend to completely remove her ventilation tube today?"

Look at me, he silently demanded. *Let me see your eyes to know if I've completely misread what I thought was mutual attraction.*

"Call me Boone, but yes, unless something has changed with her exam or vitals, then I will take her off the vent."

"Her family will be glad to hear that. Now that she's awake and wanting to communicate with them, she seems motivated to come off. As far as the other—" her long lashes swept down over pink cheeks "—that's not appropriate."

He raked his hands through his hair. "Lots of our coworkers call me Boone. There's no reason you can't do the same."

"You worked hard to earn your title. Be proud. It's not a problem for me to use your title when addressing you."

Perhaps not for her. For him, it was. Of course he was professional when they were together, but he was also a man interested in her as a woman. But she was obviously not a woman interested in him as a man. If only her eyes didn't say otherwise. Was that why she refused to meet his gaze? Because she didn't want him to see whatever shone there? Regardless, what her eyes were saying didn't matter when she verbalized a lack of interest. He had no choice but to accept her words.

"If you insist." Frustrating, but he forced a smile. "Let's go extubate Mrs. Burch."

The seventy-year-old woman was awake when he and Julia entered her room. Her husband stood beside her bed. The love the man had for his wife was obvious as he held her hand. That's what he wanted, Boone thought. A love that lasted a lifetime, through ups and downs, like the Burches had, like what his parents had. He'd not been wrong to end things with Olivia, but perhaps what he sought didn't exist for him.

"Good morning again, Irene," Julia said, flashing the warmest smile at their patient, who gave a thumbs-up as she was unable to verbalize with the ventilation tube in place. Julia then gave the woman's husband an equally bright smile. "Harry," she addressed him. "I missed you when I was here earlier."

"I went downstairs for a coffee."

"I told you I'd bring you anything you needed," Julia reminded him.

"You also told me to stretch my legs and not just sit as it wasn't good for me." The man smiled fondly at her. That Julia made the extra effort to know her patients was just one of the many reasons Boone preferred her being assigned to his patients. She genuinely cared and it showed.

"Morning," he greeted them, chatting a few seconds, then listening to the woman's chest to make sure there were no surprises prior to taking her off the machine that helped her breathe. When he was satisfied with her examination, he looked her directly in the eyes. "As you know, we've been doing spontaneous breathing trials as we wean down how much the mechanical ventilator is doing over the past few days. There's always a risk that you might have to be intubated again, but the things we watch for that let us know you're ready to come off the ventilator—heart rate, blood pressure, labs, cough strength, oxygenation and so forth—indicate that you should do fine."

Mrs. Burch gave another thumbs-up.

"What you do today is very important. Julia will be encouraging you to use your incentive spirometer to continue to strengthen your lungs and help keep them clear of secretions. Breathing deeply is vital. Your respiratory therapist will be by, as well, to work with you. Breathing without the machine is going to leave you feeling short of breath at first. Just know that's normal and focus on taking those big, deep breaths. You've got this."

Julia suctioned Mrs. Burch's lungs, removing excess secretions that naturally formed with mechanical ventilation, then stood on the opposite side of the bed from Boone, ready with a wash-cloth and to further suction the lungs as needed after he'd pulled the tube.

Boone focused on their patient, talking her through what he was doing as he could see the fear in her eyes. "You'll likely have a sore throat for a few days. That's normal and should pass," he said as he removed the tube. Mrs. Burch gagged. Julia stood at the ready to clear her air-ways. Fortunately, her gag morphed into a noisy cough.

"Coughing is important," he stressed. "Cough as needed as it's your body's way of clearing sputum."

When he felt confident that Mrs. Burch was stable, he removed his personal protection equip-ment and tossed it into the appropriate disposal bin. "I'll be back this evening to check on you." Then to Julia, he said, "Call or message me if there are any changes."

"Yes, sir, Dr. Richards," she answered without glancing up from her patient, whom she encour-aged to take a deep breath through her nose and to blow out slowly through her mouth, trying to get her to fully expand her lungs.

Boone inwardly sighed at her formality with him and the immediate contrasting warmth with which she addressed Mrs. Burch. Prior to his botched date attempt, she'd showered him with her smiles and warmth. Now she wouldn't even look directly at him. He didn't like this new cold shoulder treatment and needed to find a way to correct it. Maybe with time and patience, she'd want more. A guy could hope.

But even if she didn't want to date him, they could still be friends, because he missed her smiles and quick wit.

"Julia, I need to clear the air."

Tired from the long day, Julia eyed the man who'd jogged to catch up on her way toward the elevator that would take her to the hospital's ground floor. She let out a long sigh. Hadn't Boone done enough damage to her peace of mind already that week? She just wanted to go home, take a hot shower, eat something, and snuggle with her cat, Honey, while studying her class notes for her upcoming fall term final exams. Only one more semester to go to have her master's in nursing. She had this.

"I owe you an apology," Boone continued, and when she tried to stop him, he said, "Hear me out, please."

Curiosity getting the best of her, she slowed her pace. "Okay."

"When I asked you about the Christmas party earlier this week, I never meant to make you feel uncomfortable or pressured. Neither was my asking you to call me Boone."

"I know." That he was making the effort to say so made her like him all the more, which was not the goal. She didn't want to like Boone more. She liked him too much already.

"You've avoided me since I asked you to the party, and earlier today felt awkward, when you didn't want to call me Boone."

Yes, she had done that, and her response to the idea of calling him Boone had been very awkward. She'd always been aware of him, but thinking about anything other than him had been almost impossible since he'd asked about the Christmas party. Being so distracted the week prior to that semester's final examinations wasn't a good thing.

"I don't like the change to our interactions but do accept that it's my own fault. I'm sorry."

"Apology accepted." An apology of her own was on the tip of her tongue. Only, how did she apologize for doing the right thing? As flattered as she was by his invite, things would never work between them. Even if by some miracle he was serious, she knew they were too different. She was saving them both a lot of wasted time.

"I didn't think that my attraction to you was one-sided." He gave her a self-derisive grin. "But now that you're giving me a wide berth, I've realized I strained our friendship and our professional relationship." He gave her a look that could only be described as completely sincere. "I never intended that. You're an amazing person and nurse. I wouldn't purposely give you a reason to not want to take care of my patients or to work with me. If I offended you by showing my personal interest, I hope you'll forgive me."

There were so many things she could say. That she'd been stunned and flattered, not offended. That she knew he was a good guy, but good guys broke hearts, too. That with work, school, school clinical hours, and volunteering at the Knoxville House of Hope, she didn't have time to date. She'd vowed not to date again until after she'd graduated. Even then, she hadn't really thought she would risk doing so. After Clay, she'd imagined she'd fly through life solo.

"Tell me how I can make things right."

If ever a man had puppy-dog eyes, Boone's blue ones shone with such yearning that Julia sucked in a deep breath.

"There's no need for you to do anything to make things right beyond what you just did. We'll forget it ever happened." She wasn't admitting just how blown away she was that he was attracted to her and was making the effort to try to repair their working relationship. If things were different, she'd have been over the moon about his interest. Ha, things weren't different, and she was still over the moon. How could she not be when he'd just said he was attracted to her? Of course, he didn't know the real her, just the one she presented at the hospital, but at least that assured her she was well on her way to becoming a better person. Too bad one's past never truly went away.

"Julia?"

She glanced up, wondering if she'd made a mistake by looking into the mesmerizing blue of his eyes. She'd been avoiding doing that for fear of what he might see. She didn't fool herself that she was a good enough actress to completely hide that he wasn't wrong on his initial assessment.

"I'll try not to bother you, except regarding work. I want to get to know you better outside the hospital. I do. But I will respect that you don't feel the same."

The biggest problem with his comment was that it wasn't true. She did feel the attraction between them. The difference was that she knew the consequences of becoming involved with someone she could never truly live up to.

"If it's not too much to ask, I do have one question."

Waiting, she braced herself for whatever he might say.

"Did you answer no because you aren't interested in me? Or because I asked you to go to the hospital Christmas party and our coworkers would see us? If others knowing is what held you back, pick your pleasure. I'd take you anywhere you want to go."

Pick her pleasure. Had he really just said that? Looking at him was a pleasure. She could only imagine that touching him would be more so. *Stop it, Julia*, she scolded herself. *You don't date and if you did, you'd be a fool to get involved with someone like Boone.*

"I appreciate the offer, and certainly I wouldn't want a first date to be such a public one with my coworkers, but like I told you, I don't date."

She had to keep focused on the future. Risking that future on a man, even one as fabulous as Boone, wasn't happening.

CHAPTER TWO

THINKING IT MIGHT be best if she avoided the Christmas party altogether, Julia offered to work that night. She'd learned long ago that avoiding temptation was the best defense from giving in to things that would hurt her. Unfortunately, the nurse manager hadn't put her on the schedule. A mixture of anxiety and anticipation warred. She'd enjoyed previous celebrations with her co-workers, but she suspected she'd be on pins and needles at this year's. Maybe she should stay home with Honey.

Had Boone asked someone else to go to the party? Julia didn't plan to change her mind, but she wanted to be mentally prepared if he'd be there with someone else. Then again, for all she knew he'd gotten back together with his long-time girlfriend. Over the weeks since he'd apologized, he'd been professional, friendly enough, but definitely on guard to not overstep during their interactions.

"You're staring at the schedule awfully hard," Stephanie pointed out, coming up behind Julia to glance at the computer screen. "Oh, great! You're not working on the ninth. You want to ride with Derek and me again?"

"I'm not sure I'm going."

Stephanie frowned. "Why wouldn't you? A night to hang with the gang without the stress of worrying about our patients? You have to go."

"I really don't." Stephanie knew the highlights of Julia's past. Julia sure couldn't imagine going back to the lifestyle she'd lived during her teens, but she didn't put herself in harm's way, either. Not that the hospital Christmas party would be anything like the parties she had once frequented. Lord forbid. "I should volunteer to work while I'm in between school semesters. With clinicals, I haven't been pulled many extra hours this past semester, and I don't expect this last one to be any better. Putting back a little money over the break would be great."

Julia felt Boone vibes, signaling he was in the ICU.

"Hey, Dr. Richards," Stephanie greeted him, brandishing a big smile that made Julia nervous. "We were just talking about the hospital Christmas party. Are you going?"

Nervousness justified, Julia's face heated.

Boone's gaze briefly touched upon her. Then he looked toward Stephanie. "That's the plan."

Stephanie's elbow nudged Julia's shoulder. Julia ignored her friend and continued to stare at the computer monitor that had morphed into screensaver mode with the hospital's logo.

"Derek and I are picking up Julia." Stephanie gave another one of those smiles that hinted her news should mean something to him. "You'll have to look for us. We're a lot of fun, aren't we, Julia?"

Julia could feel Boone's gaze and fought looking toward him. Closing the computer screen, she pushed back her chair and stood. "I mentioned that we'd see about my going and whether I'd want a ride."

"Come on, Julia," her friend beckoned. "You'll be done with finals and will be between semesters. The timing is perfect to celebrate finishing up and to get you into the Christmas spirit."

Julia wasn't anti-Christmas, but the holiday held more disappointment than happy memories. These days, holidays meant earning double-time pay and volunteering to work to make the most of that opportunity.

"You're in school?" Boone's gaze burned into her, making Julia's face even hotter. She was very proud of what she was trying to achieve, but she wasn't one to go around talking about it, either.

"She's working on her master's," Stephanie supplied. "I'm so proud of this girl. Smart and beautiful. She's stressing about finals, but don't be fooled. She's acing her classes. She always does."

Julia gave her friend a look that said, *Thank you, but please don't do this*. A beeping noise sounded in Stephanie's pocket, and Julia was grateful for the interruption.

"Oh, that's me. Good to see you, Dr. Richards." Stephanie took off toward her patient's room.

"I didn't know you were in school." Boone sat down in a chair near hers behind the nurse station desk. He obviously wasn't going to steer clear of personal topics that day.

"Why would you?"

He sat there a moment, then ran his fingers through his hair, slightly rumpling the silky locks. "I promised I wouldn't bother you, so I won't respond by saying that I'd like to know."

Unable to keep from looking his way, she met his gaze, saw the sincerity and couldn't help but marvel. "Why?"

She wasn't sure whether she asked why he wanted to know, or why he was looking at her with genuine attraction shining in his eyes.

"It's not a secret that I'm interested in knowing more about you, Julia. I asked you to go to the Christmas party. Admittedly, that wasn't my most brilliant move. You were right that the party is too much under coworkers' eyes for a first date."

She nodded. Even if she had been interested, she'd never have agreed to being under a microscope on a first date.

"I hadn't thought that one through. We'll chalk it up to the fact that it's been a long time since I've asked anyone to go on a first date. I'm a bit rusty on dating etiquette. If I had it to do over, I'd simply have asked you to dinner somewhere nice, with good food and atmosphere, to just eat, talk, and get to know each other outside of work."

There wouldn't have been anything simple about his asking her to dinner. Just breathing near the man was complicated.

"That would definitely be a better plan if you intend to ask out another coworker."

He frowned. "I won't be asking out another coworker. I'm not interested in dating anyone else, Julia. Just you." He took a deep breath. "But I have a promise to keep, so we'll change the subject to work. Tell me about the new admit, Aaron West."

If ever there were a topic to remind her of the reasons why she needed to keep her eyes trained on the goal and not let anything or anyone deter her from her carefully plotted path to success, her next patient was it.

"Aaron is a seventeen-year-old male who overdosed on fentanyl-laced oxycodone tablets. Fortunately, his friends…" *if you could call them that* "…had naloxone on hand, administered it, and called for emergency help immediately." Her heart squeezed as it often did on similar cases. Cases that were flashbacks from her own past. "The paramedic administered another naloxone injection upon arrival as he was barely breathing even after being hit twice already."

Boone's expression tightened. "He's lucky his friends were sober enough to save him."

She nodded. The young man had been lucky. Just as she had once been. Unfortunately, Aaron was far from out of the woods.

"Is he responding to stimuli?"

"No. Earlier during visitation, his mother thought he moved his fingers in response to her talking to him, but there was no change in his monitor readings to indicate that it was anything more than a coincidence. His Glasgow Coma Score is seven."

"Such a waste." Shaking his head, Boone sighed. "Let's check him, and then we'll let his parents visit again."

She followed him into the ICU room. Seeing so many tubes and wires exiting her patients never failed to humble Julia and make her thankful for modern medicine. As critical as the young man was, at least he had hope of getting a second chance to make better life choices. She prayed that he would recover and do just that.

"I've looked over his notes but didn't see a history of a previous hospitalization. Is he a repeater?"

That Boone had to ask was a sad testament to how frequently the intensive care unit did have repeat overdose patients.

"No. According to the girl who called for an ambulance, he'd drunk on a few occasions but didn't do drugs. She feels confident that he only took one pill."

"That's all it takes if that pill is laced with enough fentanyl." Boone made a frustrated noise. "These pill mills put such garbage out that a single tablet can be lethal. The kid probably had no idea what he was risking. Many don't even realize some dealers lace their goods to get people hooked specifically to their product. Hopefully, Aaron will live to learn from his mistake and not suffer any long-term consequences."

Julia had been traveling the same destructive path at his age. It had taken lying right where the young man lay, a wonderful nurse, and a rehabilitation program to wake her up to the risks she'd taken. She'd been one of the lucky ones who had gotten that second chance and had done her best not to waste that precious opportunity.

"Hopefully."

That Aaron had survived the night was a blessing, but he was critical. If he survived, the next worry would be that he hadn't suffered any permanent damage from his overdose.

Boone examined him, then sighed.

"It doesn't look good, does it?" She couldn't help but ask. She usually didn't, especially not in the patient's room as one never knew what a patient was aware of, regardless of what monitors showed. But Aaron's mother weeping over him that morning had gotten to her, and Julia had been saying extra prayers all day that the young man pulled through.

Boone shook his head. "Keep it to not more than two visitors simultaneously, but let his family spend as much time with him as they wish so long as they aren't disruptive to his care or the unit. If they become a problem, then go back to standard protocol."

Grateful that he was approving the extended visitation, she nodded. With one last heartfelt glance toward the young man whose pale chest rose and fell thanks to his life support, she followed Boone from the room. "I'll talk to his parents and let them know."

He paused, pressing the sanitizer dispenser. "Those are tough, aren't they?"

Watching him rub his hands together with the disinfectant, Julia blinked. All their patients were tough. In most cases, each one was a life that impacted many others. Did he ask the question because he'd heard something about her past? Or was he just making conversation and she was being paranoid? Boone knowing just how many mistakes and poor choices she'd once made, well, the thought made her feel raw and exposed.

"I had someone close get messed up with drugs," he continued, a faraway expression on his face. "She was a star athlete, good grades, beautiful. Her entire life ahead of her just waiting to be lived. She lost everything to her drug habit." He shook his head as if to clear a memory. "I've never understood how someone could mess up their life over getting high."

"Getting high is rarely the true reason people overdose." His misconception was a common one. Doing drugs was about so much more than getting high. Depression, anxiety, peer pressure, poor life circumstances, the list went on. That Boone's comment irritated her so much didn't make sense. Maybe it was because she expected him to know better. She suspected he did know better and had just been musing out loud while frustrated by his memories. She also suspected that she was being overly sensitive because it was him, and she was grasping at any reason to like him less.

His gaze flickered to her. "I certainly don't believe that kid meant to overdose."

Julia didn't believe the young man had meant to, either. He'd given in to peer pressure and been very unlucky that he'd gotten a pill laced with enough fentanyl to overwhelm his naive system.

"Ultimately, he alone holds the responsibility for making the choice to take the drug."

"I suppose."

He eyed her a moment. "Did I upset you just then, Julia?"

"No. Maybe. It doesn't matter," she answered, feeling flustered. She put her hands beneath the dispenser and got a large dollop of the cleansing gel, so much that the alcohol scent burned her nostrils. Trying not to sniffle, she rubbed her hands together. "My point was that you shouldn't judge others unless you've walked in their shoes."

"Agreed, and neither should you," he surprised her by saying.

Not that he wasn't right. She was judging him unfairly. Obviously, she was grasping at anything she could to put up a defensive barrier against how he affected her now that he was single and had expressed interest. She was desperately seeking character flaws.

"For the record, I appreciate your protectiveness of your patients and the wonderful care you give them and their families. It's one of the first things I noticed about you when I started at Knoxville General." His tone was gentle and hinted that there was a lot more he'd like to say. Instead, he glanced at his watch. "I'm headed to the clinic. Let me know if anything changes. Have a good day, Julia."

"Uh, yeah, you too." She bit into her lower lip, watching as he headed toward the unit's double door exit. He had her insides twisted into knots.

If she ever was going to waver from the life course she'd set for herself, Boone Richards would be the reason. But she wasn't going to, no matter how much what she saw in his eyes tempted her.

"Wow. That red dress looks fantastic on you, and those gold bell earrings are so festive with their red bows."

Feeling self-conscious, Julia smiled at her nurse manager, whom she had bumped into almost immediately upon entering the Sunsphere ballroom with Stephanie and Derek. The gold glass sphere on a high tower remained from the 1982 World's Fair. It overlooked the city and was her favorite place to attend events. It looked especially beautiful tonight, decorated with deep evergreen garlands and trees adorned with gold ribbons and ornaments. The crisp air even smelled of balsam, although Julia was certain the greenery wasn't real.

"See, I told you that you look gorgeous," Stephanie reminded her. "I've never been one who could pull off a headband and am completely jell of the one holding back all your glorious hair."

Why had Julia left her heavy curls down? For that matter, why had she paid such close attention to her appearance? *Why ask questions I don't want to know the answers to?* She wasn't fooling anyone, especially not herself, by styling her hair loosely about her shoulders rather than pulling it back in its usual tight ponytail.

"Thank you," she told Patti. "I feel a little over-the-top since I rarely wear anything beyond mascara, tinted sunscreen, and lip gloss."

"Which is fine for work, but at a Christmas party?" Patti lifted her drink glass. "Go for glam. Besides, it's fun to dress up on occasion."

"She's right. You're gorgeous, Jules. Someone is going to eat his heart out that he didn't ask you to be his date." Stephanie whispered the last bit, then gave her a one-armed hug. "Oh! There's Kevin, Rob, and Becky. I'm glad they got here early and snagged a good table close to the dance floor. You want something to drink?"

"A water would be great." Julia spotted their friends, waving as they motioned her over. She really did love the crew she worked with at Knoxville General. Julia headed toward where they sat and complimented them on how they cleaned up out of their scrubs, trying not to blush too brightly when they did the same about her new-to-her secondhand store dress. It appeared brand-new and fit perfectly. It spoke volumes that she'd gone shopping with Stephanie for a new outfit rather than wearing her go-to black dress that she usually pulled out for special occasions. Volumes she didn't want to hear because they played a beat she'd rather not give in to any more than she already had.

Her insides got a quivery sensation. She'd not spotted Boone on her way to the table, but he was obviously somewhere close. Or maybe she felt that vibe because she'd been thinking of him.

"Don't look now, but your favorite doctor is on his way over here," Stephanie teased, handing a glass of water to Julia as she slid into the chair next to hers.

Knowing Boone was headed her way had her taking a deep breath. She couldn't even argue that he wasn't her favorite doctor. He was.

"Mark my words, after he sees you tonight,"

her friend continued with a brow waggle, "he's going to want Santa to deliver you on Christmas morning. Ho-ho-ho."

Julia rolled her eyes. "You're crazy, but I love you anyway."

Stephanie grinned. "Now that he's single and knows you're single, my friend, he's not going to be able to resist asking you out."

"How does he know I'm single?" Not that she hadn't pretty much told him when she'd said she didn't date, but she'd never breathed a word of that conversation to her friend. Stephanie would have been all over a juicy morsel like that.

Her friend's painted pink lips curved. "I may have mentioned it."

Julia cringed. "You shouldn't have done that. You know I don't date."

Unfazed, Stephanie's gaze didn't waver. "Only because the right person hasn't asked."

"That's not my reason. You know my reasons. I have too much going on in my life to date Boone." Not to mention that he was way out of her dating pool league. She still didn't understand why he'd asked unless it was merely to scratch a sexual itch.

"Boone, is it?" Stephanie teased. Then, seeing Julia blush, her eyes widened. "Seriously? Is that why you look like a million bucks tonight? Because you have a secret Christmas stocking stuffing rendezvous planned with Dr. Richards? Girl, I'm thrilled for you."

"Shh," she hushed her friend, shifting in her chair to where she could see Boone. Dr. Vaughn had intercepted his path to their table and was introducing him to his wife. Boone laughed at something the intensivist said, and Julia's heart hiccupped. Wearing dark slacks, a crisp red shirt, and a green tie with a pattern she couldn't quite make out, Boone stole her breath. Not that he didn't in scrubs. He was gorgeous, but it was more than that. Perhaps the warmth of his eyes, his genuine smiles, or how he truly cared about his patients.

His gaze shifted toward her and, catching her looking at him, his brow lifted in question. No wonder. She'd told him no and yet, even if he were blind, he couldn't possibly miss how he affected her. Yeah, he wasn't the only one with questions. She had them, too. Like why was her heart flip-flopping in her chest, and why did looking at him make her a little dizzy?

After a moment, he seemed to come to some conclusion, one he obviously liked based upon his grin, which was so big that Julia gulped. Heaven help her. Heat radiated from her insides to her immediately clammy skin. Ugh. She needed to keep her eyes anywhere but toward him. Glancing back at her friend, she saw

Stephanie's grin was almost as big as Boone's had been.

"Admit it. You like him."

"There's no denying that Dr. Richards is an attractive man." *Understatement of the year.* "What's not to like? He's smart, funny, kind, and a seemingly decent human being. But he's also the hospital's star pulmonologist who just got out of a long-term relationship with a gorgeous orthopedic surgeon. For all we know, they got into a tiff and will work things out."

"Maybe, but I don't think so." Taking a sip of her drink, Stephanie considered her. "He's asked you out, hasn't he? Say what you want, but I've seen how he lights up when he spots you and vice versa. He wants you, Julia, and I'm convinced the feeling is mutual."

Julia hesitated too long.

"You, my friend, are crazy. Every single woman at the hospital is all agog since he's become Knoxville's most eligible bachelor. You've been holding out on me. Not only has he asked you on a date, but you obviously shot the poor man down despite the fact that the air threatens to ignite when you two are near each other. We need to get your head examined." Stephanie's expression grew dramatically concerned. She glanced toward where Boone still talked with Dr. and Mrs. Vaughn as she asked, "Is there a doctor in the house? Doctor? Doctor? My friend needs medical attention. Maybe some mouth-to-mouth to get oxygen to her brain."

Julia grabbed her friend's hand, lowering it to the table. "My head is just fine, but I'm worried about yours." It was all Julia's other body parts that were the problem. "Let's not talk about Boone," she urged as, catching her gaze again, he excused himself and joined them.

Standing opposite her side of the table, he chatted with their coworkers, who greeted him heartily before he was able to say something directly to Julia. No wonder they were happy to see him. He was a friendly, likable guy. His baby blues met hers, and desire flickered there. She couldn't label it any other way. That he appreciated her dress-up efforts was obvious. Try as she might, she couldn't help but be flattered by that look, by the smile that slid onto his face, by his interest. If only she believed his interest wouldn't vaporize if he had a glimmer of what lay beneath her carefully constructed shiny surface. Still, the way he looked at her warmed her insides, boosting a feminine confidence that had long ago been diminished.

"Red is your color," he complimented her when he moved to stand near her and Stephanie, "but then, I've never seen you wear anything that didn't look great."

Unable to hold that sparkly blue gaze, she glanced across the glitzy room that was becoming more and more crowded. "Thank you. You clean up nicely yourself."

Oops. Had she just said that out loud? Stephanie's snicker warned she had. Cheeks warm, Julia pretended a fascination with the handful of couples sashaying on the dance floor. The hospital had hired a great local band who played a mix of country and pop. Julia loved to dance, but rarely went out. She appreciated that she'd be able to have fun with her friends tonight.

"Derek wants to grab food from those scrumptious-appearing buffet tables before it gets too crowded in here. You want to go with?" Stephanie gave Julia an out if she wanted one. Knowing her friend probably wanted to question her further, Julia shook her head, then wondered if facing her friend's inquiry might be preferable to remaining with Boone.

"Thanks, but I'm good." Her stomach was way too nervous to put food into the mix of flip-flops, anyway.

"Oh, I do. I'm starved." Becky popped up from across the table. "Save our seats, Julia?" she asked as everyone else stood, too, leaving Julia trapped there until her coworkers returned.

When the others had gone, Boone slid into

Stephanie's chair. "I'll give her seat back when she returns," he promised. "Having fun?"

"We've not been here long, but everyone seems to be having a good time."

His brows rose. "We?"

"I rode with Stephanie and Derek."

"That's right. I recall her mentioning you were riding with them."

She took another drink. "How about you? Is there someone waiting for you to get back to her?"

Why didn't she just lift her not secondhand but splurged-on shiny red heels and stick them into her mouth? Her question was as obvious as his had been. Her stomach knotted tighter. What was wrong with her?

"I came alone as it wouldn't be fair to have brought someone when I'd rather be with you."

She sucked in a breath. He was such a great guy that she wished she could just throw caution to the wind and say she'd love to go on a date with him. But she couldn't.

"Don't clam up on me, please. That was just an honest answer to your question. You've told me you don't date, and unless you've changed your mind, then we'll just be friends."

Just be friends with the most attractive man she'd ever known when he was also attracted to her? Easy-peasy. Not.

"I—I can do that." Maybe. Goodness knew she'd done tougher things over the years, so surely she could manage keeping her relationship with Boone compartmentalized.

"I never doubted your abilities." His gaze didn't waver. "So, as friends getting to know each other at a company Christmas party, tell me more about yourself. How long have you worked for Knoxville General?"

"Since nursing school graduation." Answering his question shouldn't make her feel as if she were lowering her defenses, but where Boone was concerned, the more he knew, the more exposed she felt.

"Which was?" he prompted.

"Two years ago."

"Which makes you twenty-four?" he guessed.

"Twenty-seven," she corrected him.

His brow lifted again. "Which means you graduated from nursing school at twenty-five. What did you do prior to nursing school?"

His question was a natural one, but she couldn't prevent her muscles from tensing at what the most honest answer would be, that she had more empathy for Aaron West than most could ever understand.

"Odd jobs here and there." Which was the truth. She'd done just about every odd job she'd been able to find but had never been able to hold on to any of them until she'd gotten clean. "I waitressed, worked at convenience stores, in retail, bagged groceries." She shrugged. "Whatever I could find that paid my bills. I wasn't picky."

Intrigue flickered on his face. "You were putting yourself through school?"

The school of life.

"I did work to put myself through school." She just hadn't started her nursing education straight out of high school. "Why are you the one asking all the questions?"

"Ask anything you want."

Fine. Let him be the one to have to come up with answers. She'd much rather go on the conversation offensive than discuss her past. "When did you graduate?"

"I finished residency in May."

"Knoxville General is your first nonresident position, then?"

He nodded.

"I'd ask where you went to med school, but I recall hearing right after you started that you attended in Memphis. How about your residency? Where did you do that?"

"Philadelphia."

"Is that where you're originally from?"

"I'm from West Tennessee. That's why I chose to go to school in Memphis, so I could be close to home during undergrad and medical school. My dad and brother are both physicians who work for St. Jude's, and my mother manages a shipping company that's been in her dad's family for over a hundred years."

Not surprisingly, his background sounded quite different from Julia's. Doctors and a multi-generational business. The closest thing to a multi-generational business in her family was that as a teen she'd bussed tables at bars where her mother worked.

"You're close with your family?" she asked.

He nodded. "My mom is one of my best friends. She's tough, but fair. I can tell her anything. We chat or text most days. My dad and brother are great, too, but I am admittedly closest to Mom. I would've returned to Memphis except Oliv..." He paused, seeming to weigh how much he wanted to say. "As you know, I'd been in a relationship for several years, and we mutually decided that Knoxville better suited our immediate future."

"That sounds serious." Curiosity, not jealousy, twisted her stomach.

"It was. We met in early med school and dated for five years."

"What happened?" The question slipped out, and she started to retract it, but he shrugged.

"I'm not sure anything happened. Maybe our interests changed, or we grew apart, or perhaps it's just that we were never right to begin with.

Don't get me wrong. She's great, but continuing in our relationship when I knew we had no future seemed unfair."

"You're the one who ended the relationship?" She'd wondered, thinking maybe if he'd been dumped, that played into his interest in her as a trial run to fluff his ego back up.

He nodded. "Not quite two months ago. I didn't want to hurt her, but it was for the best when we weren't right together."

He'd been single just over a month when he'd asked her about the Christmas party.

"Five years. That's a long time to be with the wrong person." Not that Julia would know. Other than Clay, she'd never been in a relationship for more than a few weeks at a time. In the grand scheme of things, her relationship with Clay hadn't lasted so long, either, but it had been long enough to break her heart. He'd been different, a good man with morals and…and he'd found her lacking. Sometimes she wondered if she ever would be good enough when her past held so much bad. "I'm sorry it didn't work out."

Boone and Dr. Cunningham, not her and Clay.

Boone nodded. "Me, too. She's a wonderful woman, and I have no regrets about the time we spent together. But I don't want to continue in a relationship that for some time had felt like a stepping stone to where I'm supposed to be in life."

A gorgeous orthopedic surgeon who by all accounts was as brilliant as she was beautiful and who he'd just called wonderful wasn't the right woman for him, but he'd asked Julia out? Had he lost his mind? If she'd said yes, how would he have someday described a relationship with her? A pebble in his shoe on the journey to where he was supposed to be in life?

"More questions?" he prompted when she didn't immediately ask another.

"Not really." She already knew enough to understand that she and Boone came from two different worlds. Pretending otherwise would lead to heartache.

"Good, because I have another for you. When you said you don't date, was that a nice way of telling me no, or do you really not date?"

"With work and school, I don't have the time or need the distraction of dating." It's the answer she'd been giving for the past five years because it had been that long since she'd been in any type of personal relationship. Since Clay.

"Notcd, but you have to eat. Surely the occasional dinner date wouldn't be a problem."

"Going on a date with someone implies that you have an interest in them, that you're willing to make spending time with them a priority. My interests and priorities are committed elsewhere."

Looking thoughtful, he eyed her. "You mean school?"

"My job and school come first. I have a life plan and find success comes more readily when I stick to it. No dating until I graduate."

"After you finish graduate school? You plan to date then?"

If she met a man who could forgive her past and keep her strong when she felt weak. If she met a man she could trust enough to reveal the horrible things she'd done, and know he wouldn't use those weaknesses against her during the normal ups and downs of a relationship. He wouldn't judge her harshly, and could see how she was working diligently not to be that person anymore.

She suspected any such man would need to have gone through something similar to truly understand, forgive, and love her. Most days she struggled to do those things herself. Mindlessly, she stroked her thumb over the tattoo on the inside of her left wrist. She was a better person than she'd once been. She was.

"Maybe."

Boone leaned back in his chair and flashed another smile. "It's good to know there's hope."

Surprised, she blinked. "I won't graduate until May."

"So, what you're saying is that I picked the wrong holiday when I asked you to the Christmas party, but you'll gladly be my date to the hospital's Memorial Day picnic?"

Her stomach somersaulted. "We discussed that a work gathering was a terrible first date."

"That's right. We did." His grin had her heart pounding. "Glad you caught that. We'll need to have gone out a few times prior to being under the work family's curious eyes." His expression grew thoughtful. "You'll have celebratory lunch plans with your family, but how about I take you to dinner on the evening of your graduation? That's usually the first Saturday in May, right?"

Celebratory lunch with her family? Her mother had passed long before her college graduation. Her father had lived out of state and hadn't chosen to attend the ceremony. She had no reason to think he'd be there when she walked the line for graduate school. What would it be like to have Boone to celebrate her successes with? No. No. No. She didn't need to let her thoughts go there. She took a sip of water to moisten her dry throat.

"That's six months away," she said.

"Time flies." He didn't seem fazed. "I'm calling dibs."

Dibs? Surely he was teasing. But although he was smiling, sincerity shone in his eyes.

"You plan to wait six months to take me on a

date? I should hold you to that," she threatened, heart pounding because she couldn't believe he was even saying such nonsense. No way would he wait for her. Not that she wanted him to. She didn't really have a plan on when she'd start dating, or even if she would. She just knew that she wouldn't while in school to avoid anything that might distract her from success.

"Good, because I intend to hold you to our graduation day date. I know I did a train wreck of a job when I asked you to this party, so let me get the next one right." He gave her one of his lopsided smiles. "Julia, will you give me the honor of taking you to dinner to celebrate earning your Master of Science in Nursing degree in May?"

Why did his question feel like so much more? As if her entire life depended upon her answer.

"You'll have long forgotten wanting to take me to dinner by then."

He shook his head. "Not a chance. My memory's good, and some things are worth waiting for."

"A date with me being one of them?"

"Definitely. Until you graduate, we'll be co-workers and friends." His eyes sparkled more brilliantly than the Christmas lights flashing across the room. "After that, we'll take one day at a time and see what happens. Deal?"

"I— Okay, one day at a time is how I live my life, anyway." There was no point in arguing with someone who was obviously certifiable. Time would prove her right, so why waste breath trying to point that out? Despite what he'd claimed, he would forget all about his impulsive invitation long before her graduation.

If only she could.

CHAPTER THREE

LEANING BACK IN his chair, Boone watched Julia laugh as she grapevined and twirled in a popular line dance with Stephanie, Becky, and a group that mostly consisted of women. Held away from her face by a wide red band, her hair fell long and luscious about her shoulders. He'd never seen her hair down because she always kept it up at the hospital, and his fingers itched to tangle in the thick silky strands to see if they were as soft as they appeared.

"I'm topping off our drinks. You want anything?" Stephanie's boyfriend, Derek, asked. Boone hadn't previously met the real estate broker who Stephanie had met when he'd sold her a house a year or so back and they'd hit it off.

He shook his head. The man couldn't deliver what Boone wanted. "I'm good. Thanks."

Rather than walking away, Derek gestured toward where Boone stared at the dance floor. "Stephanie really likes Julia, says she's been through a lot, is a great nurse and friend. For whatever it's worth, she also says that Julia likes you."

What things had Julia been through, and had she told her friend that she liked him or was Stephanie making assumptions?

"She's such a cheery little thing most of the time. I really like her, too, and have tried to set her up with a few friends over the years. She always shoots that down, saying she doesn't date."

Good to know that it truly wasn't just him.

"She's mentioned that a time or two," he admitted. He'd keep that she'd agreed to go out with him to celebrate her graduation to himself. He'd seen the distrust in her eyes when she'd said she should hold him to his dibs claim. She'd only agreed because she fully expected him to have changed his mind. He couldn't imagine that being the case. There was something different about her, something in the way he felt when he looked at her, when their eyes met, when he saw her smile, in how she was strong, and yet made him feel protective. He wanted to know more.

"We have our annual group Christmas ski trip planned to Gatlinburg over New Year's weekend. Ober Mountain's ski slopes aren't huge, and the snow is mostly machine-generated, but they're close, and we always have a great time. What could be better than good food, good friends, and fun memories, right? You're welcome to join us."

"Julia's going?"

Derek grinned. "She has the past two years, and her name is on our list. If she tried to cancel, Stephanie would drag her anyway. She says it's one of the few times Julia takes off work to do something that isn't school- or volunteer-related."

Saying yes was on the tip of his tongue. If Julia wasn't in the picture, he'd have agreed without hesitation, but what if she'd rather he not infringe upon her time with her friends? She had just agreed to go on a date with him half a year down the road, but that didn't mean she'd want him as a constant addition to her outside of work activities.

"I'll check my hospital schedule, but I'm off on New Year's." He'd planned to go home to ring in the New Year with his family. His parents always threw a humdinger of a party, but he'd be home during their more intimate Christmas celebrations. The holidays were hard on them all, but especially his mother. Sometimes he suspected that was why she threw herself into such elaborate celebrations, to distract from things she'd rather not think about. "When do you need to know by?"

"Anytime over the next week or so should be fine." Derek pulled out his phone. "Dial your number so that you'll have mine. When you know for sure, shoot me a text."

Boone did so, then handed back Derek's phone. "Thanks. I'll save it in my contacts. I visited Gatlinburg over the summer for a day hike at Mount Le Conte, but my friend and I didn't make it to Ober. The trip sounds like it will be a good time. I'll let you know."

"Sure thing, man. Now, my advice is for you to get out there and dance. Chicks love that."

Boone gave him a skeptical look. He could line dance—hey, he'd been in junior high once upon a time, and the skills he'd learned back then had seen him through his university days. But he'd stay where he was. He didn't want to end up driving away Julia by pressing too hard.

Patience was a virtue.

She glanced up, met his gaze, then misstepped, bumping into Stephanie. First apologizing to her friend, she moved back into line and didn't look his way again. Boone stayed seated, enduring Derek and the other guys' good-natured ribbing with a smile when they returned and called him out on where his attention stayed. Fortunately, they honored the bro code when the ladies rejoined them at the table and never let on that they'd been ragging him nonstop about his fascination with Julia.

A slow song came on.

Stephanie tugged on Derek's hand. "Come on, big guy. I want to dance with you."

Kevin and Becky joined the other couple on the dance floor, along with Rob and the phlebotomist who was smiling up at him with adoration, leaving Boone and Julia as the table's sole occupants. She stared straight ahead at her water glass as if she was afraid to look up.

"No pressure, feel free to say no, but would you dance with me, Julia? As friends?"

To his surprise, and maybe to her own, she nodded. Boone did a mental high-five as he stood, and they made their way to the dance floor. Unlike the other slow-dancing couples, Julia didn't melt against him, but Boone wasn't complaining. How could he when she'd placed her hands around his neck, touching him for the first time, and sending his pulse racing?

That he was so aware of her light touch, that it was the first time they'd been skin to skin, spoke volumes about how much she affected him. Or perhaps it was the zings shooting through him at their innocent touch making that so clear. Julia poured gasoline over him, then set him on fire. Did she have any idea just how much she got to him? Breathing in her soft vanilla scent had him wanting to lean close, to nuzzle into her tresses and fill his lungs with her very essence. His hands loosely at her waist had him longing to pull her flush and feel every inch of her pressed to him.

Boone swallowed the lump in his throat. "You looked like you were having fun line dancing. You're good."

She kept her gaze averted, staring at his chest. "Other than in the privacy of home, it's been last year's Christmas party since I've danced, so thank you. I didn't know some of the newer songs, but it's amazing how you just fall into step when the ones you know play."

"Like riding a bicycle. Once you've got the basics mastered, the rest just comes naturally."

Still not glancing up, she smiled. "I guess so."

They moved in silence for a few minutes, Boone enjoying having Julia in his arms and wondering how he couldn't have realized sooner just how attracted he was to her when it was so obvious. How had he worked with her for months and not acknowledged what that excitement at seeing her meant? Now that he'd touched her, there was no denying anything. At least, not for him. He wanted her and would be as patient as he needed to be.

He said, "Derek invited me to go to Gatlinburg over New Year's weekend."

She stiffened.

"I haven't given him an answer. I didn't want

to do that without talking to you first. I won't go if you don't want me to."

Her throat worked. "You don't need my permission."

"No, but showing up at your getaway with friends isn't cool without discussing it with you first to be sure you're okay with my being there."

She hesitated, seemingly thinking about what he'd said. "Why wouldn't I be okay with you being there?"

"Avoiding each other would be difficult on a trip where we are all staying in the same cabin."

"Oh. That's true." Although she kept her grip around his neck light, her arms tensed. "You want to avoid me?"

"It's more a case of the opposite. I keep promising not to push and yet, if I go, I'll struggle to stay away from you. If you don't want me there, I'll tell him I can't make it."

"I…" She repositioned her hands. "That's not fair to you. I'm an adult. We both are. If Derek invited you and you want to go, then you should go."

"It wouldn't bother you for me to be there?"

"We work together, Boone. Whether you go on this trip or not, it's not as if we aren't going to be seeing each other on a regular basis. My saying you shouldn't go would seem silly."

"Away from work is different. I don't want you to feel pressured."

"I appreciate that. You going to Gatlinburg on a group trip that you were invited to isn't you pressuring me."

But he could see her mental wheels turning, could feel the tension in the arms around his neck. Was she rubbing her thumb over the bird inked onto her left wrist? He'd noticed her doing that from time to time over the months since they'd met. "You're sure?"

"I'm not a delicate flower, Boone. You going to Gatlinburg is fine."

In some ways, Boone knew she told the truth. She was strong, and yet there was a fragility within her. A fragility that he needed to handle with care. "I'll let Derek know that I'll go."

She nodded, then with a deep breath added, "For the record, if you've met someone or gotten back together with your girlfriend, it's okay if you bring her."

"What?" Did Julia really think he might get back with Olivia? "Ex-girlfriend, Julia. We won't be getting back together."

Regardless of what happened between him and Julia, the future didn't hold anything other than the possibility of friendship with Olivia.

"Well, I didn't want you to feel awkward or as if you couldn't come if that happened. You're not the only one who doesn't want the other to feel pressured. Truly, it would be fine if you brought someone. Actually, you should."

Realizing she was serious, he sighed. "I hope you feel differently about that someday, Julia. That someday you won't be fine at the thought of my dating someone else. You'll want all my dates as your own."

Her gaze lifted to his and, looking into her big brown eyes, he wondered if maybe she hadn't been quite as serious about his bringing someone else as he'd thought. Because there was something in those honeyed depths, a yearning that called to every bit of him. A very vulnerable yearning that said she'd like to want all his dates but wouldn't dare let herself. Who had put that distrust there?

"For now, I'm going to count my blessings that the most beautiful woman here is in my arms and that I'll get to say goodbye to the old year and welcome the new with her in a few weeks— as her current friend and future graduation day date. Life is good."

Her feet stopped moving. She stared up at him with those eyes that held such wonder, with such uncertainty in what he said evident on her face, that he longed to kiss her to put all doubt to rest. But then, she gave the slightest nod. "I—yes, life is good."

Boone wanted to know what was going through that brilliant mind of hers, but as she relaxed against him, he held his questions and cherished the feel of her cheek against his chest, her fingers at his nape, and her thumbs gently brushing along his hair there. Was she even conscious she was doing that? He didn't think so.

The first Saturday in May. Yeah, he could be patient when he had to, but her graduation couldn't come fast enough. If she changed her mind between now and then and wanted a pre-graduation celebration, well, he'd be a happy man.

"What a great Christmas party!" Stephanie greeted Julia the following morning.

Glancing up from the computer screen where she'd been reviewing her nursing notes on Aaron West, Julia smiled at Stephanie. "I half expected you to call out of work today."

"Yeah, yeah, so maybe I had a little too much fun last night." Rubbing her temple, her friend sank into an empty swivel chair at the nurse station. "But admit it, the party was the best ever."

Although it was probably a mistake to do so, Julia nodded. "I had a good time."

Coming to life, Stephanie clasped her hands together. "I knew it. I wanted to jump up and down when you two were dancing."

Julia rolled her eyes. "I'm glad you didn't. That would have been all kinds of embarrassing."

"You looked so happy. Dr. Richards did, too. How many songs did y'all dance to? Five? Six? I've never seen you do more than line dance and had no idea you could swing and spin that way. Y'all looked like y'all were having a blast. Even Derek commented on it. Did Boone ask you out again?" Her friend blasted her with questions so quickly that her last sentence came out breathy. "Please tell me you said yes."

"Stephanie, I'm not going to date Boo— Dr. Richards." Because Julia wasn't counting on his being single half a year down the road. Last night it would have been impossible to miss just how many women had made a point to come over to talk to him, a few of them even asking him to dance, which he'd politely declined.

"Derek said he invited Boone to go with us to Gatlinburg."

Heat flushed Julia's cheeks. "Dr. Richards mentioned that."

Stephanie's smile was huge. "This is going to be the best trip yet. Oh, and we'll have to make sure he knows to bring a white elephant gift for our Friends-mas."

A long weekend spent with Boone away from work. As friends. She could handle being his friend—maybe. But if he was as wonderful as he'd been the night before, how would she resist the temptation in those baby blues? In his smile? It had felt wonderful to lean against him, and to pretend that she belonged in his arms and might have a happily-ever-after of her own someday. Who got that in real life?

Hands shaking, Julia logged out of her patient's chart, then stood. "I imagine Derek will let him know about the gift exchange. The more the merrier, right? I'm going to check on Aaron."

At the mention of the young man, Stephanie allowed the subject change. "His parents are just the sweetest. I ran into his dad in the elevator on my way up to the floor this morning."

"Yes, they are wonderful. You can see how much they love him. They've barely left the hospital since his admission. His mother stayed last night and is still in with him."

Julia went to the ICU room, disinfecting her hands prior to entering, and pausing just inside the doorway to take in the various tubes and lines attached to Aaron. Without them, he wouldn't survive. With them, she prayed he got strong enough to no longer need their life-extending capabilities.

While chatting with his mother, Julie checked him, making sure all lines and settings were as they should be, and recording the readings in his electronic medical record. She was still working in Aaron's room when Boone arrived. He smiled at Julia, but almost seeming nervous, he greeted the young man's mother rather than giving Julia a chance to respond. But if he had, what would she have said?

Good morning. I barely slept last night because I couldn't stop thinking about you and I really wish that wasn't the case.

Yeah, she was glad that he'd immediately focused on Mrs. West.

"Good morning, Mrs. West. How are you holding up?" He chatted with her a few minutes, then examined Aaron. "I'm decreasing Aaron's sedation today."

"And then he'll wake up?" the boy's mother asked, her face full of hope.

Boone shrugged. "I wish it was that simple. It is possible that he will awaken, but his brain may not be ready to wake up yet, and he may remain in a coma. If you recall, he wasn't conscious prior to our giving his body time to recover."

"Has it healed enough for you to decrease his medications, then? Should we wait longer? I want him to wake up, but I don't want to rush things if there's a risk it might hurt him."

"The sooner we can successfully get him off the ventilator, the better. He's reflexively moving to certain stimuli, and his EEG is indicating increased brain activity with stimuli. His progress has been slower than we'd hoped for, but I believe he's strong enough for us to start decreasing his sedation. As far as if he wakes up or how he will do—" he sighed "—that's something I can't say for sure at this point."

He answered the rest of her questions. Then he and Julia walked out of the room, pausing outside the door. "I wish I could give her better reassurances."

"You were honest." Julia rubbed her palms together with sanitizer. "I'm sure she appreciates that."

"Is her husband here? I was surprised he wasn't with her."

"He went home last night to be with their other kids. Stephanie said she rode up in the elevator with him, so he's likely in the waiting area. Some family friends had stopped by."

"I'll go talk to him." Boone paused, glancing her way. "They have two other kids, right? Both younger? It's so difficult on the entire family when something like this happens, especially at this time of year. I'm glad he went home to spend time with their other children. Hopefully, Mrs. West will soon. It would be good for them all."

Something in Boone's voice caught Julia's attention, just a nuance to his tone, but a definite inflection of emotion that made her unable to look away.

"He tried to get her to go home, but so far she's refused to leave for fear something will happen while she's gone." Julia's heart squeezed. "They live in Maryville," she continued, "so at least it's not too horrible of a drive for him to go back and forth."

"Do you have family close, Julia? It just occurred to me that although you know I'm from Memphis, I have no idea where you're originally from."

"The South."

He arched a brow. "You're purposely being vague?"

She'd found that few people ever asked her to elaborate on the answer she always gave. She should have known Boone would be one who did.

"Not really," she admitted. "We moved a lot. Pinning down one place would be difficult as none of the places we lived ever felt like home. The South is the most honest answer I could give."

"I see," he said, but she doubted he did. It was better that he didn't. No kid should grow up as she had. "Did your dad travel for work?"

"You could say that. He changed jobs frequently. My mother did, too." She reached out to the hand sanitizer, squirted another generous amount onto her palm, then rubbed her hands together more vigorously than was needed. Nothing wrong with double disinfecting, and she needed to be doing something with her hands. "My parents divorced when I was small. I lived with Mom most of the time with only the occasional visits with my dad." There were also the times she'd ended up in foster care until her mother could get herself pulled back together when child protective services had been unable to track down her father. Julia would have been better off had the state never given her back to Leah Simmons or Julia's father. She'd been happy with a few of her foster families but had never gotten to stay long enough to feel as if she belonged. Maybe she wouldn't have no matter how long she'd stayed.

"I'm sorry."

For a moment she thought she'd said her last thought out loud, but she hadn't. Still, Boone looked at her with such sympathy that she cringed and straightened her shoulders. "Lots of kids have divorced parents. It's not a big deal."

"It is when you're the kid whose parents are no longer together. I could see on your face that it wasn't easy on you."

His softly spoken comment reached inside and uncovered that mostly-by-herself kid she'd once been. She'd been four when her father had left her mother for the final time. Her home life had never been idyllic, but she hadn't known that. She'd just known that one day her father was there and then he wasn't. Her mother had gone a little crazy after he'd left. But her mother had always teetered on the edge. Julia had been seventeen when she'd died. It had only been after Julia had hit rock bottom herself that she'd begun to understand why her parents had made the choices they had. She wasn't sure she'd ever fully understand, though.

She forced a smile and hoped Boone couldn't really see beyond that facade.

"I was young and barely knew anything else. It's fine."

Her parents' divorce had been one of the easier things she'd dealt with where her parents were concerned. Fortunately, she'd buried those demons long ago.

Mostly.

Julia tried not to get too attached to her patients, but always felt vested in each one's outcome. The nature of working in the ICU meant her patients had a higher risk of not surviving, but she did all she could to will each one well.

Aaron West got to her more than most. Each day she came to work, she'd hold her breath when checking to find out how he'd fared since she'd last clocked out. He continued to improve little by little but hadn't awakened and was still dependent upon the ventilator for life-giving breath despite attempts to wean him.

"Good morning," she greeted the young man's mother on Christmas Eve morning. The woman looked as tired as she had when Julia had told her goodbye at the end of her last shift a few days previously. "Have you been home at all since I was last here?"

The woman nodded. "Geoff insisted I go home, shower, and spend some time with the other kids while he stayed with Aaron."

Julia was glad. Being at home, remembering life outside the hospital, was important for Aaron's mother's mental, emotional, and physical health. "I know your children were glad to see you."

The woman nodded. "It's just so hard to be away from Aaron. What if something happened and I wasn't here? What if he woke up and was all alone, or what if…" Her voice trailed off, and she visibly trembled. "I know I need to spend time with my other kids, too, especially with the holiday. I want to, but I need to be here. I hope they understand it isn't that I love Aaron more. It's just that he needs me more right now, you know?"

Julia hugged the woman she'd grown fond of since Aaron's admission. Oh, how she prayed for this family. "No one expects you to stay here 24/7. It's okay if you go home at night, sleep in your own bed, hug your children, but I do understand your fears about leaving Aaron's side. I've heard everything you're saying many times. What you're feeling is completely normal under the circumstances."

"Geoff wants me to go home tonight since it's Christmas Eve, for us to both be at home with our other kids. I'm so torn." The woman gave a weak, watery-eyed smile. "I don't know how you do what you do. You and all of Aaron's nurses have been so wonderful." She glanced back toward her son. "He looks better than he did during your last shift, don't you think?"

"He does. He's definitely fighting to get better. You have to stay strong so that you can help him when he does wake up. He's going to need your love and support."

The woman squeezed her son's hand. "I know."

Julia changed out his feeding bag and recorded his intake.

On her way out of the room, she ran into Boone. "Oh! Hi."

He grinned. "Hi back at you."

Awkward, she thought. Awkward. Awkward. Awkward. Because he was grinning down at her and she was smiling up at him as if…as if something was happening between them.

Nothing can happen between us.

Not just because of her vow not to date until after she'd graduated, but because she wasn't sure how she'd survive being involved with someone like Boone when it eventually ended. She didn't kid herself that it wouldn't end. Probably if she'd agreed to go out with him, he would have already lost interest. Maybe she should just…no, she shouldn't agree to go out with him. What she should do was just tell him everything, so he'd lose interest that way. Why did that thought twist her stomach into knots?

Focusing on what she should be doing, she filled him in on Aaron instead.

"I'd hoped he'd be off his ventilator long before now," Boone mused. "The longer he's on it, the harder it's going to be. We've got to get him weaning down. Is his mother with him?"

"She is."

"Poor woman. That kid never gave a thought to how many lives his taking that tainted pill would impact."

"Speaking of tainted pills— Room two has a consult for your services. The patient is a twenty-five-year-old female who overdosed during a fishbowl party last night."

Boone frowned. "Not a good way to spend the holidays. Why do people do such mindless things as dumping medications into a bowl and then blindly taking them?"

Julia could have listed the reasons, but just said, "She's a repeater and was here about ten months ago, also for an overdose."

"Two overdoses in less than a year. That doesn't bode well for her future." He sighed, then almost sounding angry, added, "You'd think she would have learned to make better choices."

"If only it was that easy."

Boone gave her an odd look, as if maybe she'd let too much of her personal emotions into her comment. His eyes shone with curiosity, but he just nodded. "Listen to us trying to solve a problem that's much bigger than us and our ICU. Thanks for the update and for being such a strong patient advocate. I'll check Aaron, and then I'll be in to examine the new admit."

Later that day, Boone held out a Christmas present toward Julia. He'd hoped to make her smile, but her frown contrasted sharply with the jolly Santa Clauses on her scrub top.

"What do you mean, this is for me?"

The past couple of weeks had been good, not back to the way things had been prior to his asking her to the Christmas party, but better. Now there was an anticipation running through him that he'd eventually know what it felt like to have

Julia look at him as more than just her friend. He'd swear she already did, so maybe his anticipation had more to do with her acceptance of what was happening between them. An acceptance that sure wasn't showing on her face currently.

Had he messed up in buying her a gift? While shopping for his family, he'd toyed with the idea of giving her a present. Once he decided, he'd put a lot of thought into figuring out what that gift would be. Although he'd have liked to shower her with presents, he'd known she'd balk if he went overboard. He'd thought himself quite clever when he'd made his purchase.

"It's Christmas Eve. We're friends. Friends give each other Christmas presents, Julia."

Not surprisingly, she clasped her hands and nervously brushed her thumb across her tattoo. "Did you buy anyone else on this unit a Christmas present?"

Patting himself on the back that he'd anticipated she wouldn't want to be singled out, he nodded. "Of course. They're my friends, too, right? Like I said, friends give each other Christmas presents."

Her brow lifted, and her big brown eyes gave him a suspicious look. "You bought them gifts? For real?"

He grinned. "For real."

"Then I guess it's okay, except I didn't get you anything, so it doesn't feel right." She eyed the present hesitantly.

"I didn't give anyone anything with the expectation of a return gift. Everyone on the unit works hard and has been great to me since I started. I wanted to show my appreciation. What better time than Christmas? Besides, haven't you ever heard that it's better to give than to receive?"

"I've heard that, but you shouldn't have done this."

Maybe, but he was glad he had, especially as curiosity shone in her eyes. He couldn't wait to see her expression when she saw what he'd given her. Would she laugh as he'd intended at the first gift? And the secret small box inside the larger one, well, although he'd meant to keep what he spent on her in line with the others' presents, it had reminded him of her, and he'd given in to temptation. After all, it was Christmas.

"You're the third person to tell me that today." He handed her the gift. "Here, take your present. No strings attached other than friendship. Giving it to you makes me happy, okay?"

Holding the gift as if it were something fragile, or perhaps as if the box contained something toxic, she cut her gaze toward him. "Three people? You should take a hint."

"I like giving presents."

"That's very kind of you, Santa."

Grinning, he gestured to the box. "This one is a little self-serving. Open it."

"Right now?" Her eyes widened, and then she shook her head. "I couldn't. I'm on the clock and should get back to work as it is."

He wouldn't risk her getting into trouble by insisting. Not that he believed she would. But she obviously didn't plan to open the present with him watching, so he sighed with exaggeration. "Okay, but you'll have to let me know what you think."

"I would have sent you a thank-you text, anyway."

That he didn't doubt. He'd be hard-pressed to name a more polite person than the pretty brunette in her red Christmas scrubs with the silly Santas smiling at him.

"I'm having visions of my family complaining because I keep checking my phone to see if you've messaged yet and I somehow missed hearing it." He grinned. "Better open it early so I don't get in trouble. Mom has a rule about our phones not being out during get-togethers, which isn't easy when there are three doctors in the family."

Her gaze lifted. "You're going to Memphis tonight?"

"I wouldn't miss being with my family on

Christmas." Her stunned look surprised him. Had she thought he wouldn't go home for the holidays? Since his sister's death, spending time with family was more important than ever. Part of him was still a little guilty that he'd miss New Year's with them. "The whole family does our best to spend major holidays together. That isn't always easy as doctors, but even during residency, my brother and I managed to be home for Christmas morning. I'm heading that way as soon as I finish here."

"Knoxville to Memphis after working all day," she mused. Genuine concern shone in her eyes. "That's what? Around a six-hour drive? Be careful."

That concern shone in her eyes pleased him more than such a simple gesture should.

"If I get sleepy, I'll call a friend to keep me awake."

"With driving from one end of the state to the other, it's going to be late by the time you arrive in Memphis. Depending upon the time, you might no longer have that person as a friend." She cleared her throat with emphasis. "Perhaps you should stop for coffee."

Boone laughed. "You have a point. Unless I get stuck in traffic. I wouldn't expect I-40 to be too bad on Christmas Eve, so I should arrive by nine. What about you? Big plans for tomorrow?"

Rather than answering, she averted her gaze, making him even more curious as to how she planned to spend her day, but also cognizant of how she'd just walled up.

"Sorry, I wasn't trying to pry—well, actually I was," he admitted, wanting to be as honest with her as he could. "If you weren't busy, I could wait to leave until you finish your shift so you could go with me to keep me awake during that tedious section of I-40 between Nashville and Memphis."

Her jaw dropped and her skin paled. He immediately regretted his offer. He wasn't sure why he'd even made it. He sure hadn't planned that one. Bringing a woman home for the holidays would certainly have livened things up. His family was still grieving his breakup with Olivia, and he'd no doubt hear all about how crazy he'd been to end the relationship. He disagreed. But if Julia would have gone, he'd have brought her with him and faced their curiosity. Gladly.

"What am I saying? Of course, you're busy. It's Christmas Day." He gestured toward the gift box again. "Enjoy that, and I hope you have a great holiday, Julia. Merry Christmas."

CHAPTER FOUR

THAT NIGHT, JULIA eyed the present Boone had given her as if the box held a rattlesnake. If not for the fact that he'd given her coworkers gifts, too, she would have refused to take the pretty package. She probably should have, anyway. But it was Christmas, and the truth was, curiosity got the better of her. She needed to know what the box held. She was even more curious about his invitation to go with him to Memphis. Had he been serious, or had that just slipped out, one of those random, casual things people say without thinking? What would he have done if she'd said yes, she'd go home with him for Christmas? How would he have explained her unexpected presence to his family?

Either way, she really did have plans. She was volunteering at the Knoxville House of Hope. The people there deserved a Christmas, too. She'd play a small role in helping to make that happen, and later that day she'd be covering a shift at the hospital.

After arriving home, she went through her normal routine: love on Honey, shower, eat, do a little cleaning in her apartment. But her insides were anything but routine. All because her gaze kept wandering to the present on her living room coffee table. What had Boone gotten her? He truly had given their coworkers thoughtful gifts. Gifts that said he knew who they were as individuals. Nothing expensive, just presents that were a testament to what a kind and observant person he was.

Just because he was nice did not mean she needed to give in to his charm, though. It was a reason why she shouldn't. Boone's upper-crust world was very different from her own lowly beginnings. Men like him didn't fall in love with women like her. Not outside of fairy tales.

Not that she wanted Boone to fall in love with her. She wasn't looking for that with any man. Not really. She liked her life, liked how she could depend upon herself, how she had picked herself up from the ashes and now was a worthwhile member of society. She wouldn't easily let anyone threaten the peace she'd worked so hard to achieve. Yet she couldn't deny that Boone did more than threaten her peace. With a mere smile, the man had her insides all shook up and tempted her to toss her Rules for Life Success notebook.

Picking up the cat brushing against her leg, she hugged the calico close and sat down on the sofa. "What do you think, Honey? Should we open this so we can quit obsessing about what's inside?"

The cat purred.

"Yeah, that's what I was thinking, too." If she opened the present tonight, then she'd be present-less on Christmas Day because she and Stephanie had already exchanged gifts, and the rest of her work crew held their Friends-mas white elephant exchange at their weekend getaway but didn't otherwise do gifts.

The cat wiggled free of her hold, but only so she could turn for Julia to stroke her back.

"Decisions. Decisions. I can open it tonight, but having something to look forward to on Christmas morning would be fun, wouldn't it?" Something that felt like it should be normal and yet was so unfamiliar to her. She couldn't recall ever opening a present on Christmas.

So instead of ripping into the shiny paper, she picked up her remote and clicked on the television. Flipping through the channels, she settled on a Christmas special she'd seen numerous times, but it was one of those shows that she could watch over and over and still enjoy. A show about hope, family, and Christmas miracles.

A little misty-eyed from the movie, Julia jumped when her phone beeped, indicating a text. Thinking it was probably Stephanie, she opened her messages.

Julia's breath caught.

"So far, so good," she read aloud, staring at the selfie of Boone sitting in his car.

His lips were stretched in a big smile that revealed his movie-star-perfect teeth. The man really was too beautiful to be real. Not that she was biased, because what reason would she have for bias? He was just a coworker and friend and future date if he truly stuck around the next six months.

She shot back her reply.

Do not text and drive!

Although judging from the background, he appeared to be parked.

I agree. I'm sitting at an electric vehicle charging station. I'm in Nashville, so about halfway home.

Halfway home. What would it feel like to have a home to travel to at the holidays? To have people anxiously awaiting your arrival and to be excited when you walked through the door, greeting you with hugs and kisses? People who called you family? She'd probably never know firsthand, but obviously, it felt good enough that Boone was willing to drive six hours for the experience.

She texted back, blaming her nostalgia on the sappy movie she was watching.

Be safe.

Will do. Did you open your present?

Tomorrow is Christmas. I'll open it then.

No need to tell him how tempted she'd been.

You're a woman of great discipline.

Then, before she could respond, he sent:

Merry Christmas Eve, Julia. I hope Santa is good to you.

What would he say if she told him that his gift was the closest thing she'd have to Santa being good to her? Ugh. How whiny and pathetic was she tonight? She was happy, had a good life, and was on track to have an even better life.

She strove to make a difference to others every single day and was blessed to have that opportunity. Life really was good.

You, too. Julia hugged her phone to her chest. Then, realizing what she was doing, she put the phone next to the present on the coffee table. She'd obviously lost her mind because no way should she allow herself to get caught up in whatever Boone was signaling with the present. She was flattered. But she knew better.

The following morning, she got ready to go to the center, fed Honey, and opened the presents she'd wrapped up for the cat, who curiously inspected what she was doing. "Catnip. Toy. Treats. Aren't you a lucky girl? Because I'm positive you weren't that good."

The cat plopped down on top of the torn paper and licked her paw.

"You're welcome." Julia laughed. Then, eyeing her present from Boone, she picked it up and gave it a gentle shake. Something small rattled inside the shirt-sized box.

"What am I doing? It's Christmas morning. Just open it already." She removed the ribbon, then carefully tore the paper and lifted the box lid.

Beneath a few layers of red and green tissue paper, she saw a wall calendar and a smaller wrapped present. The smaller box was what had rattled. Julia picked up the calendar. The funny doctor jokes on each page made her smile, as he'd probably intended. Flipping through the pages, she read one silly pun after another. When she came to May, she paused. He'd handwritten a note on the first Saturday.

Swallowing the lump in her throat, she read aloud, "Celebrate graduation with Boone."

He'd scribbled a few other notations on key dates. "Memorial Day picnic with Boone." "July Fourth fireworks with Boone." "Labor Day picnic with Boone." "Halloween party with Boone." "Thanksgiving with Boone." "Christmas with Boone."

Ah, that's what he'd meant about the gift being self-serving. He'd penciled himself into all major holidays that followed her graduation.

She eyed the smaller box. Then, a bit breathless, opened it, revealing a velvet jeweler's box inside. What had he done? With shaky hands, she lifted the lid to reveal a white-gold phoenix curved around a diamond pendant on a thin chain.

As with the gifts he'd given their coworkers, her gift had been personal, had reflected that he knew who she was, or in this case who she strove to be—a phoenix rising from the ashes of her crash-and-burn life.

With moisture prickling her eyes, she reminded herself that he was a doctor. Buying a piece of jewelry was no big deal to him. He'd obviously noticed her tattoo and thought the pendant would be something she'd like. Only, that he'd chosen something so meaningful…

Julia sniffled. No. No. No. She could not be bought. Not that the piece was an overly expensive one. At least, she didn't think so, but what did she know about jewelry? She never bought real, and this was the first piece she'd ever been given. Once upon a time she'd dreamed Clay would buy her something special, but that dream had been quickly crushed.

Part of her considered setting the necklace aside to give back to Boone, but another part won. The part that thought it was the most perfect pendant she'd ever seen and was completely wowed by his insight. She removed the necklace from its box, put it on with trembling hands, then went to the mirror to look at her reflection. The intricately cut stone encircled by the phoenix reflected the light and seemed to catch fire within the sparkly depths, perhaps a sign that her good intentions would soon do the same.

"You are in so much trouble, Julia Simmons," she warned herself. But neither the warning, nor her discomfort at his gift, was enough to wipe away the joy spreading through her. She couldn't imagine any gift that would mean more than the beautifully designed pendant.

Impulsively, she picked up her phone and took a funny-faced selfie.

I hear this used to be coal. Does that mean Santa thinks I've been bad this year?

Squeezing her eyes closed, she hit Send. What was she doing? Now she'd be a nervous wreck that she'd texted him. What if he didn't answer? Would she be the one continuously checking her phone? What was wrong with her? A well-to-do man had given her a piece of jewelry that meant nothing to him beyond that he'd noticed her tattoo. Still, she'd promised to thank him. Her message hadn't quite been that, but...

Ugh, why hadn't she just sent a simple thank-you, and been done with it? Why did she always end up doing more where Boone was concerned than she should have? What was it about him that continually pushed her so far beyond her comfort zone?

Her phone beeped, and with heavy anticipation, she looked to see what he'd written.

Perfect.

Relief filled her that he'd messaged back. The necklace did look perfect. It must feel perfect, too, because she couldn't quit touching the pendant. How could a piece of jewelry delight and terrify all at the same time?

Her phone beeped again.

The necklace isn't bad, either.

A smile spread across her face.

Ha-ha. You're a funny guy. I absolutely love it, but it was too much.

He was too much.

I am a funny guy. It wasn't too much. Did you like your calendar?

You need to return it. Someone has scribbled on several pages.

Picking up the calendar, she flipped through the pages again, pausing when her phone beeped.

You know how doctors' handwriting can be. One scribble after another.

Apparently... Thank you, Boone. Your gifts are very thoughtful.

I didn't want you to forget.

As if she could.

Besides, like I said, the calendar was as much for me as it was for you. The necklace is your gift. Although it would seem that ended up being as much for me, too.

She reread his message, trying to decipher what he meant. When she couldn't decide, she asked him.

How so?

I can't think of a better gift than seeing your face.

Julia had friends who'd been wooed in the past, but she had never been the recipient of anything beyond someone buying her a beer. She couldn't help but wonder if this was how it felt to be wooed, to have a decent man want to date you. Clay had been a decent man in many ways, but he'd never been able to get beyond her past, had never been able to see her as capable of rising above who and what she'd been. Nor had his family. No matter what she'd done, she hadn't been good enough in their eyes. Clay had cared about her, but that hadn't kept him from walking away. Julia touched the pendant, pressing it into her chest and wondering if the jewel would leave a mark as it burned intensely against her skin. Boone was just making conversation. He was just generalizing and being his usual complimentary self. His words didn't mean anything, and yet, they puffed her chest.

She typed back, although she wasn't sure how to respond. Did he have any idea how thoroughly he affected her?

That drive must have really gotten to you last night.

Scrolling back a few texts, she found the selfie he'd sent her the night before. Handsome, smiling, and such a good person. Seriously, he wanted to date her? Maybe she'd fallen and was dreaming it all. That was it. She'd been watching television the night before, had dozed off, and was having a dream miracle on her street.

The drive wasn't bad and was worth it to be home for Christmas.

Before she could respond another message arrived.

My mother has a breakfast feast this morning and has invited the entire Richards and Hemingway clans for dinner tonight. The house is in literal Christmas chaos.

Visions of smiling people celebrating the holidays together danced through her head, contrasting greatly with her own Christmas memories.

He continued,

It's a good thing we're texting because you wouldn't be able to hear me for all the background noise. I'd forgotten how loud my family is.

Clenching her phone, she took a deep breath. Enough of this silliness. She needed to get ready to spend the day with the only family she had outside of work.

I've got to go, but thank you. The calendar made me smile, and the necklace is beautiful beyond words. You shouldn't have.

Closing her eyes, she hit Send. She knew better, but she'd be lying if she didn't admit to being flattered. Even if only for a brief moment in time, Boone Richards was attracted to her. If nothing else, that was a rosy testament to the person she painted herself to be. If only she could recolor the past and truly soar so high no one could look down upon her.

It would help to stop getting distracted by a gorgeous man who seemed to say and do all the right things.

Stick to your rules, Julia. You have them for a reason.

Her phone beeped, and she glanced at his message.

Merry Christmas, Julia.

Merry Christmas to you, too.

Then, eyeing the cat, who had followed her into the bedroom, she sighed. "I'm in trouble, Honey. I have this next portion of my life planned out. If I'm not careful, Boone Richards is going to derail those plans, and I'm going to be left dealing with the wreckage."

She'd almost backslid when Clay dumped her. How could she risk going through that again? How would she survive if it was Boone who found her lacking when already she recognized that he affected her in ways Clay never had?

"What has you smiling so big?"

Boone glanced up from the dining table and flashed an even bigger smile at his mother. "It's

Christmas morning, and you've got all my favorite foods served. Why wouldn't I be smiling?"

"Right." His mother rolled her eyes, but her smile was genuine when she gestured to his phone, "What's her name?"

He never could get anything by her. "Whose?" he asked anyway, but with a grin.

"Whomever you were texting with. Not Olivia, I assume." She gave him the same patient look she always had when they both knew he would end up telling her what she wanted to know. He imagined that look had been perfected over the years of running the shipping business. No wonder the business had flourished under her guidance since she'd taken control after his grandfather had passed.

"You assume correctly."

"I didn't think so. As much as I liked that dear girl and know that she would have made you an ideal wife, I'll admit you have a sparkle in your eyes now that I like seeing." She took a sip of her coffee. "When will we meet this new woman in your life?"

Good question, and one that he didn't have an answer for. Just because Julia had said yes to his taking her out to celebrate her graduation, that didn't mean she'd go along with the rest of his penciled-in itinerary. He'd like to think she would since his gut instinct was that she was just as interested in him as he was in her. Well, maybe not that much, but she was interested.

"I might bring her home this summer."

His mother's eyes widened. "This summer? Good heavens. Surely you're not planning to wait that long before your next trip home? I expect you here for your birthday."

"I'm planning to come home for my birthday."

"But not to bring your new lady friend?" His mother gave him a stern look. "Are you afraid for her to meet your family?"

Boone snorted. "You know better than that. I invited her this Christmas, but she turned me down."

Obviously shocked that anyone could turn down one of her children, his mother regarded him for a long moment. "What kind of woman doesn't want to meet the family of the man she's dating?"

"Good point, but we're not dating." And he'd have been floored if Julia had said yes to going to Memphis with him. With all the walls she hid behind, she probably wouldn't come to Memphis with him next Christmas, either.

Looking more and more curious, his mother eyed him. "But you want to be dating?"

"I do. She doesn't." Or maybe she did but was just sticking to the plans she'd made for herself. He could respect that. Not that he had a choice.

"She's a nurse and working on her master's degree."

Curiosity shown on his mother's face. "She sounds like a smart girl."

"Smart, funny, beautiful. Perfect manners." He shrugged. "You'll like her."

"You obviously do." She set her coffee cup on the table and pinned him beneath her blue gaze. "She's why you broke things off with Olivia?"

He shook his head. "I broke things off with Olivia because we weren't right together."

"But you realized this after meeting this nurse? She refused to go out with you because you were involved with Olivia?"

Boone frowned. "I've known Julia since I started in Knoxville. I didn't ask her out until *after* Olivia and I weren't together anymore. I was single. Julia was single. I asked. She said no."

"Julia…" His mother let the name roll off her tongue. "Does Olivia know about her?"

"Whether or not Olivia knows no longer matters to me, Mom." He sighed. "Not that there's anything to know. Julia refuses to go out with me until she graduates. End of story. Our first date is my taking her out to celebrate the night of her graduation."

Her perfectly shaped brows lifted. "In May? But that's months from now."

He nodded. "It is, but she refuses to date me, or anyone, until she finishes school. She claims dating might distract her from her priorities."

"This woman wants you to wait around six months for her to graduate? What if she changes her mind between now and then? What if she meets someone else and you've wasted half a year waiting on a woman who isn't that interested in you? If she's that okay with waiting, she mustn't like you as much as you think. Not that I understand how any woman could resist such a wonderful young man as yourself, but I don't want to see you hurt."

Boone had considered that Julia might change her mind about going out with him, but he hadn't considered that it might be because she'd met another man. His chest squeezed at the thought of someone sweeping Julia off her feet despite the fact that Boone had called dibs. His calling dibs didn't obligate Julia in any way, but…he wanted it to.

"I suppose that could happen. If it does, I'll be disappointed, but since I can't imagine going out with anyone else—" he shrugged "—well, that wouldn't really be fair to whomever I was with, would it? I'll take my chances and wait."

His mother eyed him a moment, then smiled the slyest smile. He wondered if she'd been playing him with feigned shock and misunderstanding to elicit more information from him. "I look forward to meeting your Julia this summer and hope she's worth your wait."

"She is." He took a deep breath. Oh, yes, Amelia Hemingway Richards's smile was smug. "As far as this summer, we'll see. She's agreed to a single dinner date after her graduation, nothing more."

"But if you have your way, she will agree to more?"

"Definitely."

"Then, as I said, I look forward to meeting your Julia this summer."

"This is going to be the best Friends-mas getaway ever," Stephanie assured Julia from the front passenger seat of the SUV Derek drove up the steep mountain road. "And not just because it's snowing, and all around us looks like something from a holiday movie. Can you believe there are twelve of us staying at the cabin this year?"

Twelve, and all were couples except Julia and Boone. Reaching up, she touched where her necklace lay hidden beneath the neckline of her shirt. She'd made sure to wear something that covered it, but she hadn't taken it off since she'd put it on. Somehow the pendant felt as if it was as much a part of her as her tattoo.

"Did you bring the giraffe?" She changed the subject to the white elephant gift that had made a return appearance each of the past two years.

"Maybe." Stephanie laughed in a way that let Julia know her friend had. "I checked the weather, and there's real snow on the slopes, too. Yay!" With Tennessee weather, one never knew, but there were snow machines to keep the slopes operating regardless of the fluctuating winter temperatures. "We've got a great view from our cabin on Ski View Drive. I'm glad Dr. Richards didn't mind sharing a room with Cliff."

"He seemed okay with it once I assured him there were two beds," Derek added from the driver's seat, glancing briefly at Julia via the rearview mirror and grinning.

Cliff was a respiratory therapist at the hospital. Julia was sharing a room with his girlfriend, Dawn. She'd met the woman briefly at the Christmas party, and she'd been friendly enough. Cliff and Dawn had been dating a couple of months but weren't sleeping together. He'd asked if Julia would mind sharing her room if he covered half the cost. Cutting expenses was always a good thing. This last semester, she would have a lot of clinical hours, had to finish her thesis, and worried about how much she'd have to cut back her work hours. She lived low and had a decent savings account, but having been homeless at more than one point during her life, being financially secure was a big deal. She knew well how quickly things could change.

Stephanie was still chatting away when they pulled into the small parking area in front of the gorgeous mountainside cabin Derek had secured for them through his realty office. Kevin, Becky, and another couple were already there as they'd driven up earlier in the day to check in and pick up food and supplies. Julia had spent the day before baking goodies and had packed them along with Derek's cooler and more supplies in the back of his SUV.

Besides Kevin's car, there were two other vehicles already in the parking area, one of which she recognized as Boone's expensive electric car. As there was only a light dusting of snow across the top, she guessed he'd not been there for more than half an hour.

Almost as if he'd been watching for them, he appeared in the doorway just as Derek was opening the back hatch. His gaze met Julia's, and he smiled. "Hey." Then he said to Derek, "You were right about this place. The view of Mount Le Conte is spectacular. What can I carry in?"

"If you want to grab the other side of the cooler, we'll bring it to the kitchen and come back to get the rest of this stuff Stephanie insisted we needed," Derek told him.

Stephanie waved her gloved hand dismissively. "Yeah, yeah, but when you have yummy food, plus party hats and kazoos for welcoming in the new year tomorrow evening, you can thank me."

Derek waggled his brows at Stephanie. "Something like that."

Pulling her coat tighter around her, Stephanie rolled her eyes. "Men. One-track minds."

"Which you appreciate about me," Derek reminded her, handing her the suitcase that had been on top of the cooler.

Stephanie gave him an innocent look. "You think?"

"Baby, I know." He pulled the large cooler forward so he and Boone could readily grasp the handles.

As they walked off, Stephanie reached for another bag, draped the straps over her shoulder, and giggled as she glanced toward Julia. "He's right. I do appreciate that about him."

Julia reached for her own brightly patterned cloth overnight bag, a gift two years prior from Stephanie. "I'm positive I don't want to hear this."

Her friend laughed. "Someday someone is going to sweep you off your feet, Julia, and you're going to know exactly what I mean." Stephanie's grin turned sly. "Maybe even this weekend. A girl can hope."

Julia gave her a horrified look. "Promise me you aren't going to throw me and Dr. Richards together all weekend."

Stephanie shifted her overnight bag on her shoulder, then pulled up her larger suitcase's handle so she could roll it inside. "As you're the only singles, I won't have to. You'll be paired off without me doing a thing."

Bingo. Julia had known that was going to happen. She'd come anyway. What did that say?

Nothing. It meant she wasn't changing her plans with her friends just because Boone would be there, too. It meant she could be his friend. It meant… Why was her pendant burning into her chest?

"I should have begged Patti to let me work this weekend." But the truth was that she was looking forward to the trip. Obviously, she'd lost her mind.

As they made their way into the cabin, Stephanie laughed. "You working this weekend would have been a real shame. Can you think of a better way to ring out the old and bring in the new than with all of us?"

"You're forgetting how much I love my cat."

Stephanie laughed. "Honey will be just fine with Mrs. Smithfield."

Having dropped off the cooler and meeting

them at the door, Boone reached for Julia's bag. "Let me get this for you. Who's Honey?"

"My cat."

Boone took her bag, along with Stephanie's.

"You're in the room across from mine and Cliff's," he told her. "He and Dawn haven't arrived yet, so you get first choice on which bed you want. I picked the one closest to the window. The view is spectacular."

"That's sweet of you to get our bags, Dr. Richards," Stephanie exclaimed, giving Julia a knowing smile as they stepped into the cabin. "Thank you."

"Call me Boone," he reminded her. "I don't want to be called Dr. Richards all weekend."

"Do you hear that, Julia? He doesn't want to be called Dr. Richards all weekend," Stephanie practically sang as she took her bag from him.

"La-la-la... Did you say something?" Julia responded, but with a smile. "Seriously, I can finish carrying my bag to my room if you'll just point me in the right direction."

"Showing you is easier. With three stories, this place is a maze. We're upstairs from the main floor, so head toward those stairs. There are two bedrooms on that floor, one on the main, and three on the lower."

Following him, Julia nodded.

"This is you." He gestured to the doorway.

Julia stepped into the room with its wooden log walls and black bear decor. "Nice."

"Ours is similar." He placed her bag onto one of the two full-sized beds. "I'll go help Derek finish unpacking his SUV."

"I should help, too."

He shook his head. "Stay. Unpack or go warm yourself by the fire Kevin has blazing in the main room."

"I— Thank you, Boone."

At her use of his name, he grinned. "I like that."

She liked a lot about him, particularly the way he was looking at her, not sexually, although the physical tension was there between them, but with genuine affection.

"You like me showing my gratitude?"

"You saying my name," he corrected her, his smile widening.

Those eyes. That smile. Be still her rapidly beating heart. Had she majorly miscalculated this weekend? Or had she purposely not fully acknowledged how spending this time with him was going to affect her?

"Get used to it," she warned. "As the only non-couple here, we'll be paired together for every activity. I'll be 'Boone this' and 'Boone that' all weekend." She'd put up a fight at the hospital, but addressing him so formally at a gathering of friends would seem strange.

"We both know I'm good with that. However, I will ask Derek to buddy up with me if you want. I meant it when I said I didn't want my being here to make you uncomfortable."

Too late. His very existence pushed her outside her comfort zone.

His lips twitched. "I'll even do my best to not make Stephanie jealous."

"I could see how she might be," Julia teased to give herself time to process his sincerity. Stephanie would have a fit if Julia accepted his offer. She breathed in, then slowly exhaled. "I think we're adult enough that we'll be fine without you making moves on my best friend's guy."

"You think I'm adult enough?" His grin begged to differ.

"There's still time for changing my mind."

His gaze searched hers a moment. "I'm glad Derek invited me, Julia, and that you're okay with me being here."

She gave him a questioning look. "Did I say that?"

His gaze held hers, making her insides flutter like the fat snowflakes dancing outside the window. "No, but it's true, isn't it?"

Unfortunately, he was right. If something had come up and he'd canceled, she would have missed him, which didn't make sense since he never had been there in the past. How could she miss something she'd never experienced?

Including his parents' large gathering, Boone had turned down several New Year's Eve party invitations and had no regrets. Glancing around the cabin's main room at the smiling faces, there was nowhere he'd rather be.

Not completely true, he admitted, because he'd much rather be next to Julia sitting on the sofa with Stephanie and Derek. Instead he was in the kitchen chair he'd moved into the living area for their white elephant gift exchange. He'd considered placing it by the sofa but had opted for across the room instead as it put Julia directly in his line of vision.

"Who has number seven?" Stephanie looked around the room.

"That's me." Becky jumped up from the oversized chair where she'd been snuggled next to Kevin. "Hmm, do I want to take that yummy-looking cheese board from Cliff, or do I want to see what another one of these packages holds?"

Cliff hugged the gourmet cheese board gift set to his chest. "Keep your paws off my cheese."

Everyone laughed when Becky took his gift. He then opted to open another present and let out a woo-hoo at the barbecue set he unwrapped. "Nice. Who's number eight?"

"That would be me." Julia walked over to the tree and chose a gift. It was a fuzzy blanket with a black bear on it. She undid the binding and wrapped the fleece material around her shoulders. "Aww, it matches our cabin. Wearing this puts me in stealth mode."

Everyone laughed.

Kevin went next and groaned when he unwrapped Stephanie's gift. Everyone burst into laughter.

"You have to bring it back next year," Stephanie reminded him.

"No worries about that," Kevin assured her. "If I don't accidentally on purpose leave him here, this guy will be making another appearance on the mountain."

They went through the remainder of the gift-picking, and at last it was Boone's turn. As number twelve, he had his pick of taking anyone's gift or choosing the last unwrapped one. Pretending to contemplate, he eyed each gift.

"Take mine. You know you always wanted a ceramic giraffe," Kevin offered.

"I'll restrain myself," Boone told him, then moved in front of Julia. "Anyone think there's a draft in here? I feel a bit chilly."

"No!" she gasped, clasping the blanket more

tightly around herself. "You don't want this ole thing."

"I do. Hand it over." By doing so, he'd be giving her the choice of any of the gifts. He'd seen how she'd eyed the hot cocoa and mug set when Dawn had unwrapped it, and yet she'd not stolen the gift when it had been her turn. Before the weekend was over, he'd give the blanket back. That way she could have two gifts.

Sighing and faking a pout, she handed over the blanket. "I can't believe you'd take my Christmas present."

"Believe." He wrapped the blanket around himself. Julia's body heat clung to the fuzzy material, as did her vanilla scent. Instantly, visions of dancing with her at the Christmas party flashed through his mind, warming him much more than the blanket or the fire Kevin still had roaring. "Just what I always wanted."

"A bear blanket?" She shook her head, then glanced around the room. Her gaze lingered on the cocoa set that Dawn held.

"No. Don't do it," her roommate for the weekend cried.

Just when he thought Julia would take the set, she walked to the tree and picked up the last remaining package instead, ending the game with whatever was inside.

She smiled when she unwrapped a box of

chocolate-and-caramel-covered pecan candy with a department store gift card taped to the package. "This is awesome. Thank you to who-ever brought this."

"That was fun." Stephanie began gathering wrapping paper and trash from the floor. Every-one pitched in and quickly had the room restored.

Derek grabbed Stephanie around the waist and pulled her in for a kiss. "You up for a game of pool? Boone, you in?"

"Come on, Julia." Stephanie wiggled free of his hold. "We'll play partners. Girls against guys. Pool's your game."

"Oh?" Boone glanced in Julia's direction. "This I want to see. Count me in."

Julia eyed the blanket still draped over his shoulders like a superhero cape. "Winner gets the blanket."

His lips twitched. "You want to strip me of my bear blankie?"

Her brown eyes sparkled with mischief. "Turn-about is fair play."

"Assuming you'll win," he teased.

"Assuming that, of course." She arched a brow. "Do we have a deal?"

"We do." Boone was pretty sure he was being suckered, but he didn't mind in the slightest. "This thing better bring me luck."

Looking pleased with his answer, she asked,

"You're going to play while wearing my blanket?"

"You think I shouldn't wear *my* blanket?"

"We'll see whose blanket," she warned, lips twitching. "Haven't you ever heard that thing about a cape being a superhero's downfall?"

"I'll take my chances. This one is *beary* lucky."

Moving next to them, Stephanie snorted. "You better hope so, because you're going to need it playing against us, right, Julia?"

A smile upon her lush lips, Julia just shrugged as she headed toward the stairs that led down to the cabin's game room. Turning at the top, eyes twinkling with a mischief he adored, she crooked her finger. "Hurry up, Boone. I want my blanket back."

Later, hot chocolate in hand, Julia went outside to sit on the covered balcony that looked out toward Mount Le Conte. Boone grabbed his jacket and followed to sit in the rocker next to hers. An outdoor heater was lit near them, blowing warm air in their direction.

"Sure would feel better if I hadn't lost my blanket," he moaned, knowing his comment would make her smile and feeling pleased when it did. He'd always admired her cheery disposition at work, but more and more he recognized the smiles that went deep compared to the surface ones. That one had been real, and he liked it.

She glanced his way. "Between the heater, hot chocolate, and my blanket, it is quite comfy. Too bad you lost this magnificent gift."

"I can tell you're heartbroken about it." He laughed. "Where did you become a pool shark?"

She hesitated a moment, then answered, "No one place. My mom waitressed at one honky-tonk after another over the years and brought me with her until I got old enough to stay on my own. By then I often wanted to go rather than stay in whatever rathole we currently called home. I'd have to stay out of sight in the back when they were busy, but during slow times I could entertain myself with pool or darts. Regulars would let me play, giving me pointers. After a while, you learn a few things."

He didn't really like the idea of a child hanging out in bars, but he understood what she meant.

Julia turned back to stare toward the mountain. She took a sip of her hot cocoa from the package Stephanie had brought, which reminded him of something he'd been wondering.

"Why didn't you pick Dawn's gift?"

She continued to stare out into the darkness. "What do you mean? I like my chocolates and gift card."

"I saw how you eyed Dawn's cocoa gift set,"

he pressed. "It's what you wanted, but you didn't take it. Why not?"

"I knew Stephanie had brought a giant box." She held up her cup as evidence, then took a sip. "It wasn't a big deal."

"The idea of the game is to take what you want, though, right?"

"It's all in fun. Besides, what I liked best was my bear blanket." She snuggled within the blanket that dragged the floor at the rocking chair's base.

"Which I took." Not that he believed she liked the blanket better than the gift set. At least, not initially. Now he was quite fond of the blanket himself.

"Then proceeded to lose back to me," she reminded him with a smile and a lift of her mug in his direction. "Poor Boone. You ended up without a gift. Since it's Christmas, I'll share my chocolates with you."

"Nice of you. I'd planned to give the blanket back anyway."

She narrowed her eyes. "You're saying you lost on purpose?"

"For the record, I never lose on purpose."

She looked relieved. "Good to know."

"But I suspect you do." His words were quiet, but he knew she'd heard them. He'd meant her to.

Turning toward him, she frowned. A breeze

caught at her hair, and the strands danced about her face. "What's that supposed to mean? That I'm a loser?"

"You're not a loser. Far from it. It's just a hunch that you put others before yourself most if not all of the time." It was a quality that she shared with Amy, with the exception of his sister's fatal flaw. On that, he could only think Amy had been selfish, as how else could she have done the things she'd done?

Julia swatted at her hair with her free hand, brushing it back to tuck behind her ears. "Obviously, that isn't true." At his doubtful look, she reminded him, "I didn't hesitate to beat you earlier, even though such a devastating loss had to hurt your male ego."

He laughed. "There is that, but that's different, isn't it?"

She'd gone back to gently rocking the chair. "If you say so."

"So, you're a pool shark. Sounds like I should avoid playing against you at darts. Anything else up your sleeve that I should know about?"

She took another sip of her hot chocolate. "Nothing that comes to mind."

"What about skiing? Are you going to show me up tomorrow with your traversing?"

She laughed. "I'm not sure what traversing is, but if it involves falling a lot while on the kiddie slopes, then yep, that would be me shaming you on the snow."

"Not a skier?"

"I've been twice, last New Year's and the previous one. Both times I ended up spending most of my time just trying to stay upright. But third time's the charm, they say."

"Well, you do have my lucky bear blanket."

Smiling, she nodded. "There is that. Maybe I'll take a page from your book and wear it about my shoulders like a superhero cape and ski down the slopes with it flapping in the wind behind me."

He smiled at the image. "I wouldn't do that. Someone recently told me that capes were dangerous."

"Somebody was paying attention."

"Hard not to pay attention when it's you doing the talking, Julia."

Her gaze cut toward him. "Meaning I'm loud?"

"Meaning that when you say something, I'm all ears."

She snorted. "Nice recovery."

"The truth."

Taking a deep breath, she turned to look out into the darkness. "There's a lot you don't know about me."

"I look forward to discovering those things."

"You think that, but I've done things I wish I could change."

"That's true of most people."

"Even you?"

Did she think he was perfect? That he'd never made mistakes? That he hadn't been oblivious to the warning signs that his twin had started using again? That he hadn't failed to stop her from going down a path she hadn't been able to return from? He almost told Julia about Amy. Almost.

Instead, he just admitted, "Even me."

CHAPTER FIVE

The following morning, clad in neon-green-and-pink ski pants and jacket she'd borrowed from Beth, Julia wondered if she should have brought her bear blanket as a good luck charm to keep her upright. She sure needed something as she was beginning to doubt that all the four-leaf clovers in the world would be enough to accomplish her staying vertical. At this point, she'd just like to get back onto her feet. Each time she tried, her skis went out from beneath her, preventing her from standing. She had a helmet for her head, but perhaps cushioning for her bottom would have been more useful.

"Hold your feet like this and dig the edges of your skis into the snow."

She glanced up through her also borrowed ski goggles. Boone was demonstrating his instructions. He wore a bright blue-and-yellow ski jacket and pants. His helmet and goggles matched. Someone should snap his photo because he looked like an advertisement for ski fashion. "You've already made it down the main slope? That has to be some kind of record."

"When I realized you hadn't gotten onto the chair lift with us, I asked Stephanie about you. She told me you had stayed behind, so I came back."

"You didn't need to do that." Sucking in a lungful of cold air, she sighed. "I may never be ready to go up. I think I mentioned that I wasn't very good at this."

He grinned. "Only because you've not had me to give you pointers."

"Ha. Last year the whole crew tried. I never left the practice area. In the meantime, I've forgotten how to stay upright and can't seem to get on my feet. Give a girl a hand?"

He shook his head. "No. It's time you learn." With that, he purposely fell over. "Watch how I do this, and then you do the same. I'm going to show you the simplest way to right yourself."

He talked her through how he positioned his legs and skis, then used his hands to walk himself into an upright position.

She wrinkled her nose at him. "You make that look easy."

"I had lots of practice when I was learning to ski."

"How long ago was that?" She emulated what

he'd done and was quite proud of herself when she managed to stand. Now if she could just stay that way.

"Honestly? I can't recall exactly. My grandfather was a big skier, and we took a few trips every year back when he was alive. He died my senior year of undergrad. Since then, I've gone with friends a few times, but we've not done any big family ski trips. It was a rough year."

"I'm sorry. I didn't mean to bring up painful memories."

"You didn't. Those trips are good memories of happy times. Losing my grandfather and the other things that happened that year don't change that." He dug his ski pole across the snow. "Now, let's practice duckwalking."

Disliking how his melancholy affected her and how strongly she wanted to put his smile back into place, she drew her brows together. "Perhaps you missed the part where I can't human walk with these things on my feet, much less duckwalk. However, lucky for you, I'm an expert duck talker." She pursed her lips. "Quack. Quack."

As she'd hoped, he laughed. "So many talents. Who knew? Now, let's see if you're as good a copycat as you are a quacker."

Deciding to go with whatever he showed her, Julia mimicked his walking movements.

"Relax your knees," he advised.

"Relax?" She fake-laughed. "You're kidding, right? Who can relax when they have long wooden sticks attached to their feet?"

"You're doing great, Julia. Just smile and have fun with it. If you fall, no big deal. It'll just be more practice of how to get up."

Which she could competently do now thanks to his earlier instruction. "Okay. Duckwalk while relaxed."

He grinned. "That a girl. You've got this."

Not really, but after following his instructions, she was staying upright. That was a start.

He patiently walked her through several more movements, demonstrating each one, then observing her attempts and giving pointers on ways to improve. Not once did he make her feel incompetent or hopeless. Before long, her smile was real. She didn't fool herself about just why she was enjoying herself. It had little to do with the skis and everything to do with the instructor.

"It's time for us to go down the beginner slope," he announced a few minutes later when she'd semi-successfully demonstrated each of the skills he'd taught her. "Just remember to relax and keep a smile on your face."

"You got it." She bared gritted teeth in a semblance of a smile, then blew out a cold puff of air.

He laughed.

With Boone patiently skiing near her, Julia made it down the beginner slope with no mishaps. After her second successful trip down the short slope, Boone convinced her to attempt a slightly more difficult slope. She wasn't sure that was a good idea, but he hadn't led her astray thus far. She'd just go slow and do her best to stay on her feet while he skied ahead. Only, when they reached the step-up slope, Boone continued to stay close, offering nonverbal tips and pointing out the beautiful mountains jutting up to meet the cloud-dotted blue sky.

A commotion ahead caught their attention. "Someone's down. They look hurt," he called. "Just keep doing what you're doing and meet me there. I'm going ahead to see if I can help."

Picking up his pace, he skied ahead over the powdery white snow, sliding to a stop near someone lying on the ground in front of several tall evergreens.

Julia maintained her slow and steady pace because if she'd sped up, she likely would have just fallen. When she got close, she saw actually two people were lying on the ground, with Boone knelt over one. She managed to slow as he'd taught her and came to a stop several yards away. She duckwalked to him.

"Julia, this is Craig and Sylvia. He seems the more seriously injured. If you don't mind, I'm going to use your scarf to make a tourniquet on his leg to slow his bleeding while you check Sylvia."

The man was pale except for his nose, which was red from the cold. Julia handed over her scarf.

"I've called for emergency services." Boone took her scarf. "They're on speaker now. Someone should be here to help within a few minutes."

Julia quickly unhooked her skis, then knelt next to the woman, who lay awkwardly in the snow with her hand to her head. Fortunately, she wore a helmet that had hopefully prevented a concussion. "Hi, Sylvia."

The woman gave a weak smile of acknowledgment, then closed her eyes again. "Hi."

"What hurts?" Julia asked.

"Everything, but at least I'm not bleeding like he is. I wanted to try to get up, but your husband said I shouldn't."

"Coworker," she corrected the woman, but her body instantly going clammy beneath her ski gear. "I'm an ICU nurse. Dr. Richards is the best doctor I know." A pulmonologist, but prior to declaring his specialty, he would have dealt with many different medical scenarios. She didn't doubt his ability to handle this accident. "Is it okay if I touch you to check you, Sylvia?"

Keeping her eyes closed, the woman made a sound of agreement.

Julia ran her hands over her arms, making sure the bones lined up, then proceeded to check the woman's legs. When she came to the woman's right ankle, she grimaced. Although the bones hadn't broken through the skin surface, both the tibia and fibula were broken and displaced just above where the woman's boot ended.

"That hurts." Sylvia opened her eyes and reached toward Julia to stop her.

"Sorry. I wasn't trying to hurt you. Unfortunately, your leg is broken. You aren't going to be crazy about this, but I'm going to pack snow around the area," she told the woman. "It'll help to keep the swelling down."

Once she had snow around the woman's leg, she ran through a quick neuro check. Fortunately, other than the ankle and being shaken up, Sylvia seemed okay and was in enough shock that her pain was only semi-registering.

"We collided. I was skiing, and the next thing I knew, I was on the ground," Sylvia explained, apparently deciding she no longer had to remain still as she propped herself up on her elbows so she could see what was going on.

"I'm sorry," Craig said from where he lay. "I couldn't slow down." He lifted his hand to his head. "Man, that hurts, and I feel as if my glasses are digging into my face."

Julia moved closer and pushed his ski glasses

onto his helmet to look into his eyes. His pupils were different sizes. He swiped at his nose. Blood streaked across his glove.

His frightened gaze went to Julia's. "That can't be good."

"You probably bumped it when you collided." Hopefully, that's all that it was, but his dilated pupils concerned her. Maybe something more had happened.

"He really doesn't look good, does he?" Sylvia's question only made Craig look worse.

"Why did she say that?" he asked. "What are you not telling me? Am I bleeding to death?"

"Blood scares some people," Boone assured him. He was further assessing the man's leg, trying to keep him calm. If he got excited, his heart would pump faster, and keeping his blood loss down would be more difficult. But the idea that he might be hurt worse than he'd thought had Craig struggling to sit up. Julia put her hand on his chest, staying him.

"Don't. Your leg is broken, and unlike Sylvia's, your fracture cut through your skin and you're actively bleeding. Plus, you may have further injuries. It's better to rest until the emergency workers arrive to help you off the mountain." When the man seemed uncertain, Julia waved her hand in front of his face. She'd have snapped her fingers if her gloves would let her. "Look at me," she ordered.

After a moment, he focused on her. "I'm going to have to go to the hospital, aren't I?"

"You need to see an orthopedic surgeon regarding your leg."

"Can't Doc there pop it back into place?"

"Not my specialty," Boone assured him. He was back on the phone with the EMS while continuing to slow the bleeding. "I'm a lung specialist."

"Too bad I didn't break a lung instead, eh?"

A punctured lung would have come with a whole different set of worries. "I'm glad you didn't," Boone assured him, then answered the operator's question.

Face pale, Craig closed his eyes.

"Craig?"

He didn't answer. He'd just been talking to them, but something about the laxity of his expression told her something more was going on. Had he passed out?

"Craig?" She knelt next to the man. Boone had already stopped what he was doing at the man's leg to move close to his upper body, as well.

While Julia pushed his high-necked shirt down so she could reach his carotid artery to check his pulse, Boone placed his hand on the man's shoulder. "Craig? Can you hear me?"

The man didn't respond.

"He has a pulse and is breathing," Julia assured Boone. "His pupils were off from some type of head injury."

"I noticed that, too." Boone gave her a worried look. "He likely just passed out, but keep a watch. He's bleeding too much, still. I'm going to see if I can get your scarf tied tighter around his leg." He gestured to one of the growing number of bystanders who'd joined them rather than continuing down the slope. "I want you to elevate his good leg. Gently."

He did as Boone instructed.

Julia kept a check on Craig's pulse and respirations, calling over to Sylvia repeatedly to make sure the woman was still okay. She was. When the rescue crew arrived, Julia sighed in relief. She and Boone helped get man and woman loaded into the back of an all-terrain vehicle.

When the rescuers were on their way with the injured duo, Boone glanced toward Julia. "Sorry about your scarf. I'll buy you a new one."

"It's not a big deal." At this point her adrenaline had her plenty warm. "I'm just glad you were able to get the bleeding slowed. With as much blood as there was, his fracture must have cut into an artery."

Boone glanced around. The spectators had dispersed with the emergency crew's departure with the couple. "You know that what happened with them was a freak accident, right? In all my years of skiing, I've never come across anything like that. Usually, any injuries are more along the lines of strains and sprains."

Pushing her glasses back into place, Julia nodded. She was quite proud of herself considering how she'd started.

"You made a lot of progress with your skiing today. I don't want you using this as an excuse to end your lesson."

"Hmm." She pretended to consider. "I hadn't thought of that, but you do have a point."

He stared directly into her eyes as if he could see beyond her glasses and into her very soul. "I won't let anything happen to you, Julia."

She'd been teasing, but his voice held such sincerity that she gulped back the emotions hitting her. "You're saying that had I been Sylvia, you could have saved me from an out-of-control skier?"

"Even if I'd had to throw myself into the line of fire to stop him."

Julia's heart swelled to the point that she wondered if the sound of it echoed around the mountains. Had there ever been anyone in her life who would truly sacrifice himself for her? She knew there hadn't. Not even her parents had ever put her needs first. She felt overwhelmed that, in this moment, she believed he would sacrifice his own good for hers. Panic had her desperate to lighten her thoughts. "My hero. I'll have to give you back the bear-blanket-slash-cape."

He grinned. "I like that."

"That I'm considering returning the blanket?"

"The blanket is yours. I meant you thinking I'm your hero."

There he went again, making her insides all fluttery and warm despite the brisk wind. "Everyone who just witnessed what happened knows you're a hero."

His look was intense as he said, "Just so long as you think so."

"I see what a hero you are at the hospital. No worries." She had been awed from the first time she'd caught him sitting next to a patient's bed, half-asleep, and realized that rather than going home, he'd spent the night at his patient's side. Since then, he'd only continued to break down every wall she had. Resisting his charms was impossible.

How would she ever stick to her Rules for Life Success? But she knew she'd only live to regret it if she didn't.

With the exception of the duo who'd been hurt on the ski slope earlier, Boone had had a fantastic day. Seeing Julia away from work, relaxing, laughing, and enjoying life, even teasing him at times, gave him a deep sense of satisfaction. Like all was right in the world.

Everyone hung out in the cabin's rustic decor living room, watching a Times Square special as they counted down until midnight and the changing of one year into the next. The fireplace crackled and had the room toasty warm. Hot-natured anyway, he'd shed his heavier layers for a T-shirt and jeans. Julia, on the other hand, wore a thick fuzzy maroon sweater and black stretchy pants.

"We are going to make such a mess," Julia mused, toying with the confetti popper she held.

"There's a vacuum in the closet. I'll help with cleanup," Boone offered, reaching out to straighten Julia's party hat. Stephanie had insisted they all wear them.

Julia arched a brow. "Like you men cleaned up after yourselves earlier?"

Boone grinned. "Hey, I wasn't going to argue when Stephanie said that the girls would clean since the guys had done the cooking."

Julia looked skeptical. "Not that I don't appreciate y'all toughing the cold, but is grilling really even cooking?"

It had mostly consisted of them standing around the grill while wearing their outdoor gear and shooting the breeze. "You have to admit that it tasted good."

She nodded. "I'm not much of a meat eater,

but I'll grant you that those vegetable skewers were amazing."

"Topped off by the desserts you ladies brought. Those no-bake cookies you made were my favorite. I'm a fan of anything that has peanut butter."

The fire's reflection added an extra sparkle to her eyes, giving them an almost golden look. "I'll remember that in case I ever need to get on your good side."

He could assure her that she already was, but just grinned. "I can send you a list of things that would work, if you'd like."

"Aw, you're always so helpful. I'm thinking food would be at the top of your list."

"Food is always good." Truth was, she would be at the top of his list. If he'd had any doubt, spending time with her this weekend had him convinced more than ever that Julia was different from anyone he'd ever known. That being around her made him different.

"Okay, everyone get together for a group picture." Stephanie glanced at her watch, then back to where she'd put her phone on a tripod. "I can't believe another year is almost gone."

Everyone piled onto the sofa or around it. Several of the women curled up in their guy's lap. Julia went to move to the floor, but Stephanie stopped her.

"No, you two sitting next to each other is

going to throw off the symmetry of the photo when we're otherwise all girls sitting in guys' laps." Stephanie looked directly at Julia. "Sit in Boone's lap."

Julia's eyes widened. "Um…no."

"It's only for long enough for me to get a group picture," Stephanie pleaded, the others joining in. "It's not a big deal. Come on. Hurry up so we can get back to the TV before the ball drops. We don't want to miss doing the countdown."

Boone winced at the peer pressure her friends were placing upon her and settled it by standing. "If anyone is sitting in someone else's lap, I'm sitting in Julia's."

Giving him a horrified look, Julia jumped up from her seat. "I don't think so."

"Party pooper," Stephanie accused, laughing. Then she motioned for one of the standing couples to take his place. "Fine. You two win, but only because the clock is ticking. Why don't y'all move to stand behind the sofa and just lean forward."

They did so, smiling when Stephanie said to smile and making funny faces when she said to make funny faces. Stephanie snapped photos by pushing the remote control's button. "Everyone, grab your horn and blow." They did so. "Now, grab your partner and get one last smooch for the year."

The look Julia shot her friend said it all. Boone would like to have had his *first* kiss for the year, but to try to ease what could be an awkward moment, he immediately held out his hand for a friendly shake. Glancing at his offering, Julia laughed.

"That's great," she said as she shook it. Boone got to hold her hand, and though it wasn't quite a kiss, the moment wasn't lost on him, either. Holding her hand, even briefly, was something to be cherished. Mostly, though, he was glad she was smiling.

Stephanie checked her phone attached to the tripod, then motioned for them to resume positions. "One more, guys. Then we'll get our drinks ready to toast the new year and all the wonderful things it will bring."

Everyone had champagne except Julia and Becky, whose glasses had sparkling cider instead.

"Oh, look, there's less than one minute to go!" Dawn motioned to the television where the Times Square ball would soon drop.

"Out with the old and in with the new," someone said. Several said cheers as they toasted each other.

"Ten, nine, eight…" they counted down, getting louder with each number. "One! Happy New Year!"

Several couples kissed. Julia's gaze met his, and she looked away almost immediately. She hadn't been quick enough, though, to keep him from seeing the desire in her eyes. Next year, he thought. No, not next year. This year, because they'd started a new year, the year Julia had agreed to go out with him in May.

"Happy New Year, Julia."

"You, too, Boone." Her gaze dropped to his mouth. Looking a little nervous, she moistened her lips, then took a sip of her cider. "I hope it's your best ever."

"It's off to a good start." He wanted to kiss her. To welcome in the year with the taste of her mouth on his lips. He knew better, of course. Five months. Then she'd go on a date with him. They might not kiss on that date, or even the next one, but they would kiss. Of that he had no doubt. She could stick to her no-dating-until-after-graduation rule, but he wasn't wrong about how she looked at him. He wasn't alone in whatever this was between them. For now, he'd be satisfied with spending as much time with her as she'd allow as friends anticipating whatever the future held.

"You're right. It is." Her smile was such a mixture of sweet temptation and guarded uncertainty that it was all he could do to keep from pulling her to him and assuring her she had no reason to doubt his attraction.

Instead, he reminded himself that patience was a virtue, and that Julia really was worth the wait.

Julia gulped back the lump that had formed in her throat. Boone was thinking about kissing her. He was looking at her mouth and…and she wanted him to take the initiative. She wanted his kiss. But she was glad that he had self-control. If he'd acted on his impulse, she'd have regretted it when they went back to their realities.

Maybe.

Because part of her wanted to know what kissing Boone felt like. She couldn't think of a single thing that would be a better start to her year than knowing what it felt like to lose herself in his arms.

"Cheers," Stephanie called again from where she was hugged up next to Derek, pulling Julia back from whatever fantasy world her mind had wandered off to. "I want to make a toast." Stephanie waited until everyone was looking her way. "To good friends and good times."

"Cheers," they all agreed, holding up their glasses, then taking a drink.

Soon thereafter, Kevin and Becky called it a night, as did Stephanie and Derek, saying they'd clean up in the morning. Dawn said she was headed upstairs, and Cliff offered to walk her up—not that anyone believed Dawn needed to be escorted to her room, but their PDA had been in full force all evening.

Not wanting to interrupt the couple's good-night, Julia knelt to pick up bits of colorful paper rather than going upstairs. Boone began gathering confetti, too.

"You don't need to help," Julia assured him, wondering if it was a good idea for them to be alone. Not that she thought he'd pressure her. She was more worried it might be the other way around. He'd been so kind and attentive all day, had made her laugh, opened doors, and been an absolute perfect gentleman. She'd felt self-conscious at times thanks to her friends' knowing looks, but the truth was, he'd made her feel cherished, as if she were a woman worth the effort. That scared her, because she didn't expect him to stick around. What if he did? What if she had to tell him about her past? Her fingers clenched around the paper she held. What if, like Clay, he never looked at her the same way?

"I like helping you, Julia. Besides, I figure our roommates are in the hallway saying good-night. We'll give them a few minutes of privacy."

When they went upstairs ten minutes later,

Julia and Dawn's door was shut. Boone and Cliff's door was open with no one in sight.

Realizing the couple were in her and Dawn's room and might be a while, Julia gave Boone an embarrassed look. "I'm going back downstairs for a while."

Because no way was she knocking on the bedroom door and interrupting whatever was going on in the room she shared with Dawn.

"Me, too." When she started to protest, Boone shook his head. "It isn't as if I'll be able to go to sleep with knowing you're downstairs killing time. If you even get to go to bed. Cliff might not reappear until morning."

Knowing he was right, she grimaced. "Regardless, you don't have to stay awake just because I can't go into my room. I can watch television. It'll be fine. Get some rest."

But he wasn't having it. "I'm not sleepy."

She wasn't sure she believed him but nodded. The living room was empty when they went back downstairs, and the house seemed eerily quiet. Rather than turn on the television, Julia gestured to an oversized woven game board on the coffee table. "Do you want to play checkers?"

"Sure. Why not?" Then he gave her a suspicious look. "Are you as good at checkers as you are at pool? Are you trying to shame me so I'll cry myself to sleep on the first night of the new year?"

Lips twitching, she shook her head. "Lucky for you, I'm not. I'd say I'm somewhere between my pool-playing skills and my ski skills."

His eyes twinkled. "Then what you're saying is that I have a fighting chance?"

She hesitated long enough that the silence stretched between them. Then her gaze met his. "Yes, Boone. I'd say you have a chance. A good chance."

But whether she meant checkers or something more was debatable.

CHAPTER SIX

"STILL CLOSED." Julia eyed her bedroom door more than an hour later, "I could knock and order him out of the room."

"Or you could just sleep in my bed," Boone offered. He stood next to her in the dimly lit hallway.

Her brows knit together in a deep vee. They'd had such a great time playing checkers. Laughing and each winning equally. As always, the sexual awareness was there, but not once had he made any untoward move. Until now. "Boone, I—"

"Hold up. That's not what I was implying," he assured her, his expression sincere. "You sleep in my room, lock the door, and I'll take the sofa. It's huge and has that extended side. I'll be fine."

Fatigue having caught up with her long ago, Julia considered his offer, but she doubted she was tired enough that she'd sleep if she was snuggled between Boone's covers. Would the quilts smell of his spicy male scent? Would she lie there imagining him, or would she drift off and dream he was there beside her?

Stop it, Julia. Do not let your mind go there.

She bit into her lower lip. "I'm not nearly as tall. It makes more sense for me to take the sofa."

"Except that it feels ungentlemanly to sleep in my bed while you're stuck on the sofa," he pointed out. "I wouldn't rest knowing I did that to you."

His mother would be proud of his manners. Boone was a gentleman through and through, and Julia appreciated that about him. However, on this, he wouldn't win. She wasn't sleeping in his room. Something about being in a bed he'd been in the night before felt too intimate, silly as it was.

"What if Cliff returns to his room during the night?"

"Doubtful, but like I said, just lock the door. Turnabout is fair play."

She shook her head. "I can't sleep in your room, Boone."

Appearing torn, he acquiesced. "At least let me give you my quilt and extra pillow."

"That would be great." Which meant she'd soon know if his covers smelled of him. How was she supposed to sleep if he filled her senses?

Going into his room, he got a blanket and pillow. "You're sure you won't let me take the sofa? Or how about if I took Cliff's bed and you slept in mine? You'd be completely safe. I wouldn't misbehave."

"I didn't think you would."

His grin was lethal. "Ah, I see. You're worried that you might misbehave."

"You've figured me out." She rolled her eyes as if she were teasing, but it might surprise him to know that there was a part of her that longed to sleep with his arms around her. She'd never been a cuddler, but there was something about Boone that made her long to know what it would feel like to snuggle next to him while she slept. All she had to do was say the word and he'd do just that. Sticking to her rules sure wasn't easy when it came to Boone, but veering from her plan would be a mistake. "It's me who is the problem."

Truer words had never been said.

"Hey, my intentions were pure." Eyes twinkling, he held out the bedding. "Can I help it if you have a dirty mind?"

Taking the pillow and blanket from him, she gave a dramatic eye roll. "Right. I should have known you had no ulterior motive."

"I wouldn't go that far. I'm not above trying to make a good impression, though."

Did he think he had to try? She wondered this

as she creaked her way down the wooden stairway. She must be doing a better job than she thought at suppressing how he affected her. No one had ever impressed her more than Boone. What would he have done if she'd said, yes, she'd share his room? Would he have backtracked or been just fine with their friends discovering she'd spent the night in his room and thinking they'd had sex?

Squeezing her eyes closed, she inhaled the faint scent of him on the quilt around her, allowing her mind the freedom to imagine that things were different, that she'd shared a kiss with Boone to ring in the new year, that she'd had the right to take him by the hand and lead him to a room they shared, and...

She gulped, knowing she had to get her mind under control. Even if she was willing, a dalliance with Boone could completely derail everything she'd worked so hard for. Even if he didn't hightail it the way Clay had and they got romantically involved, she had no delusions that it would last.

Clay's walking away had hurt, had almost led to a relapse to dull the ache of not feeling good enough to deserve to be loved. Boone affected her in ways Clay never had. How much more devastating would it be to fall for someone like Boone and then lose him? What if she wasn't strong enough to resist dulling her heartache? She couldn't imagine ever going back on that destructive path, but she also knew how easy it was to give in to a weak moment under the mistaken guise of diminishing one's pain. How many times had she witnessed someone relapse? Too many to count. The best way to stay clean was to not put herself into bad situations.

Protecting her new life, her hard-won success, was crucial. It was everything.

She'd be friends with Boone. He was a good man. But she couldn't allow things to go beyond that friendship. She just couldn't.

Come May, if he was still around, well, she'd figure that out then.

The following day, as Boone rolled his car to a halt at a stop sign, he snuck a glance at Julia in his passenger seat. "Stephanie was pretty obvious."

"You mean on foisting driving me back to Knoxville upon you?" Continuing to look out the window at the lightly snow-covered trees that lined the road, Julia sighed. "I'm sorry you got stuck with me."

"I'm not complaining. The company is nice." After glancing both ways, he turned the car onto the Gatlinburg Bypass. "How did you sleep?"

"Not too bad."

"But not as well as if you'd been in your bed?" he guessed, not surprised that she hadn't said one word of complaint about having her room taken over. Instead, she'd assured Cliff and an embarrassed Dawn that it was okay, she understood. Boone, on the other hand, had pulled their co-worker aside and had a talk with him.

"You should have taken my offer of my room," Boone told Julia. "I felt guilty being in my bed, knowing you were down on the sofa."

"It's really okay. Cliff apologized profusely. I guess a night on the sofa is a small price to pay for a friend to be nonstop smiles, eh? Honestly, I feel badly that he insisted on covering all of my stay."

"Only fair since you didn't get to sleep in your room last night." As he'd pointed out to the man that morning during their conversation. He didn't know Julia's financial situation, but judging from what he knew about her background and graduate school, he suspected funds were tight. She shouldn't have had to pay for a room she hadn't gotten to sleep in.

"I guess, but I didn't expect him to do that and tried to refuse." Glancing out the window, she added, "Even in the midst of winter, it's beautiful here, isn't it? The views of the mountains while we were driving down were breathtaking."

She was breathtaking. "We'll come back this

spring when everything turns green." Sensing her reaction to what he'd said, he revised, "We'll come back here this summer after you've graduated, and everything is green."

Julia sighed. "Boone, I…it would be better for you not to say things like that."

His gaze shifted toward her for a second, noting how she rubbed her finger across her inner left wrist. Sometimes he wondered if that tattoo caught fire to draw her attention to it. "Because you don't plan to spend time with me this summer?"

She tucked her right hand beneath the edges of her thigh. "This summer is months away. It's premature to make plans that far in advance when neither of us knows how we'll feel."

His gaze stayed on the road, but his grip tightened on the steering wheel. "You think our first date will go that badly?"

"If we even have a first date." She sounded as if she didn't belief they would. "You may meet someone between now and then, so taking me out wouldn't be feasible."

Frustration hit. Why was it so difficult for her to have faith in him?

"I'm not looking to meet someone, Julia." He'd already met someone. Her. More and more he wished Amy were there, that he could introduce Julia to his twin, and watch the two of them bond. Amy would have adored Julia, especially the fact that she didn't just give him his way. Sadness and anger seared through him. His sister would never meet Julia, and that was a crying shame.

"Isn't that when they say you're most likely to meet someone? When you're not trying to?" She'd kept her voice light, as if her comment was teasing, but it was obvious a world of hurt was buried deep behind her inability to trust that he would be waiting until she was ready to date. "Besides, you can't know how you're going to feel five months from now."

"I disagree."

"Okay, fine. You disagree." She twisted in her seat to face him. "Let me ask you this, then. Did you know five months ago that you and Dr. Cunningham would no longer be together?"

He kept his gaze on the curvy road, but Boone wanted to look into Julia's big brown eyes to let her see the truth in what he was about to say. "My answer may surprise you, but yes, deep down, I did know that Olivia and I wouldn't be together. We dated a long time, but maybe I've always known that we'd eventually go our separate ways."

"Did you tell her this?"

Guilt hit. "As soon as I acknowledged that truth, yes, I told Olivia. She's a wonderful woman and friend. I enjoyed her company. When we first started dating, neither of us was looking for a permanent relationship. But we got along well, had a lot in common, and our relationship was easy for the both of us. Now we want different things. Continuing our relationship would have been wrong knowing that. She deserves better."

Julia straightened in her seat and stared out the window. They rode in silence for a few minutes. Then, sliding her hand out from beneath her thigh to stroke her wrist, she said, "I find all this overwhelming, Boone. I'm flattered by your interest, but I need to focus on school and work and not have to take another person into account when making decisions. Having someone in my life gives that person power to pull emotional strings that I prefer being the sole controller of. That may sound selfish, but it's how I feel."

"Not so much selfish as lonely." Had what he'd admitted about his relationship with Olivia offended Julia? Maybe he'd been too frank if she was saying she'd rather stay hidden behind her walls than take a chance with him. Honesty was important. He wanted her to trust him.

"There are things far worse than loneliness." Her tone left no doubt that she spoke from experience.

"I take it you've had a bad relationship?"

"None in the past few years and none that

I want to talk about, but I doubt many get to twenty-seven without having fallen for the wrong person at least once. I'm no exception."

Julia had obviously cared deeply for someone who had hurt her. What kind of idiot had her affections and lost them?

"If you ever do want to talk, I'm a really good listener." An older-model Chevrolet catching his eyes, Boone changed the subject as he suspected if he didn't lighten the conversation, Julia would be completely clammed up prior to their reaching Pigeon Forge. "What's your favorite car?"

Seeming relieved, she shrugged. "I've never given it much thought. I guess I'd say the one that gets me back and forth and where I need to go without any hiccups. How about you?"

"A 1955 Corvette," he answered without hesitation. It wasn't the car that had caught his eye but had been his go-to favorite since he'd been a young teen.

"Obviously you've given it some thought." She twisted toward him as much as her seat belt allowed. "So why don't you have this dream car?"

"They're pretty rare. Only seven hundred were made, and even less than that are still in existence. Purchasing one isn't practical, but they're sharp."

Her gasp was overly dramatic. "I'm in shock over here. You don't get everything you want?"

He chuckled. "You of all people shouldn't have to ask me that question to know the answer."

After stopping in Sevierville to grab lunch prior to heading back onto I-40 West, they jumped from one topic to another that included a mildly heated debate about who the all-time greatest contestant was on their favorite singing competition for the remainder of the drive back to Knoxville.

When they arrived at her apartment, Boone popped the trunk and got out her bag. "I'll carry this up."

Surprisingly, she didn't argue, just smiled. "I'll give you this, Boone. You have impeccable manners."

He grinned. "My mother would be proud to hear you say that. I told her the same thing about you."

Julia's eyes widened. "You talked to your mother about me? When? Why would you do that?"

"I mentioned you when I was home at Christmas and several times since during phone conversations. She likes you." He followed Julia up the two flights of stairs to her apartment, then stood behind her while she unlocked her door.

"She doesn't even know me." Julia gave him a suspicious look. "You're coming in, aren't you?"

Boone hesitated. He had assumed he'd carry

her bag into her apartment, but he could see how that might make her uncomfortable. "Not if you don't want me to."

She grimaced, then sighed. "It would be rude not to invite you in after you carried up my bag."

"You are not obligated to invite me in. I can put your bag wherever you like and then leave, Julia."

"I...okay." She pushed the door open and stepped aside for him to enter. "Just place it by the door. I'll unpack it after you're gone."

He stepped into the apartment and glanced around the small but tidy studio. The walls were painted a pale yellow, and everything was trimmed in white. Her furniture was a hodge-podge of mismatched items that came together in a way that worked. Colorful throw pillows on the sofa and bed added vibrant splashes. "You live here alone?"

"Just me and Honey. My neighbor kept her while I was in Gatlinburg. She brought her home this morning before she headed out. Hello, Honey, I'm home," she called, then turned to him with an almost eagerness for him to meet the cat shining in her eyes. "She is a great cat, but just know that she doesn't take well to strangers."

How many strangers does Julia have at her apartment?

"She is a sweetie, but I'm convinced she believes this is her place and that she is just graciously allowing me to live here."

Honey didn't come when Julia called, and Boone arched a brow. "You know, if Honey was a dog, she'd be licking you like crazy right now."

"True, but I'm more of a cat person."

"Why's that?"

"I'm not sure. With a few exceptions at foster homes, I never had pets growing up. I can't say that I planned to have one as an adult. It wasn't something I'd given any thought to, but when this sweet kitten showed up scared and hungry in the hospital parking lot, well, I couldn't leave her."

It didn't surprise him that she'd not been able to leave the cat, but part of her answer shocked him. "Foster homes?"

Wincing, Julia was no doubt mentally kicking herself for her revelation. "My mother battled with a few demons. Occasionally, I'd be placed elsewhere while she got her act together."

"You didn't stay with your father?" He'd sensed she'd had a rough childhood but hadn't realized just how rough. Had her mother battled the same demons his sister had? Had that been how she'd died, too? No wonder Julia was such an advocate for their overdose patients getting appropriate post-hospital treatment.

"Sometimes. Sometimes not." She shrugged as if it were no big deal, but her voice was a little higher-pitched than normal when she called, "Honey? Where are you?"

He wanted to ask more about her childhood, to tell Julia about Amy and how he felt as if there were a hole inside him at losing his twin, but he didn't. They'd had too good a day to upset her. "So, where did the name Honey come from?"

"Not long after I brought her home, a television show was on while I was doing homework, and a character said, 'Honey, I'm home.' For whatever reason, the line resonated, and I started doing the same when I'd walk in the door. The name stuck." The previously sleeping cat rose up from beneath the pillows on Julia's bed. She'd been so nestled in them that he hadn't noticed her when he'd been scanning the room. "Here she is. Hello, Honey, I'm home." Julia picked up the cat. "How is my good kitty?"

Boone watched her love on the cat a moment and felt silly at the jealousy that hit him at how freely she bestowed her affections.

"Did you miss me? Hmm?" She rubbed her cheek against the cat's face. Honey meowed and nuzzled Julia. "I missed you, too. Do you want to meet my friend, Boone?"

Her friend, Boone.

Why did his heart skip at the description? He wasn't even sure if it was a positive or negative skip. Was he excited she considered him a friend or worried about the label when he wanted so much more? No way did he want to be permanently friend-zoned. Was that even a possibility with the chemistry between them? Sometimes when their eyes met, he'd swear the air sizzled.

Boone waited for Julia to indicate that he could pet the cat. Fortunately, the cat didn't hiss, scratch, or bite him when he gave her a gentle stroke. "Nice kitty."

"She likes you." Julia sounded surprised. "She usually doesn't like strangers, and particularly not males."

Like her owner. That Julia had taken in the cat and allowed the furry critter to steal her heart made Boone smile.

He had hope.

"Nice scrub top. Does that mean you have Valentine's Day plans for next week?"

At Stephanie's question, Julia glanced up from the electronic medical record she was reviewing. "Thanks. Candy conversation hearts are rather iconic, aren't they?" She recalled getting a few tiny boxes of them when in grammar school and meticulously going through them to read each little heart. The candies hadn't tasted very good, but she'd always been excited to read the messages each year, almost as if she'd expected some great love revelation. "I found the top last summer when we went to that thrift store, remember? And, yes, I have Valentine's Day plans."

Leaning over the desk that separated the area from the hall, Stephanie let loose with a squeal. "For real? You're going out with Boone? Yay! I knew it was only a matter of time. That's so wonderful."

Tucking a stray hair that had escaped her braid, Julia sighed. "That's not what you asked me. You asked if I had plans for Valentine's. I do. I'm working until the end of my shift. Then I'll be at home studying for a test later in the week."

Stephanie's disappointment was palpable as she scrunched her face. "Let me think, go on a date with a gorgeous doctor or study for an exam that we both know you're going to ace—girl, you have your priorities all wrong."

Julia's priorities were where they needed to be.

"I ace my tests because I study. And for the record, Boone hasn't mentioned Valentine's to me, nor should he. We aren't a couple," she reminded Stephanie for what felt like the millionth time since Gatlinburg. "We aren't dating. We are coworkers and friends. The sooner you accept that, the better."

"We had such a great time over New Year's, and you two got along beautifully. Don't bother denying it. If I hadn't seen you there, I've seen you here since. You both light up when the other one is around. Not that you didn't before our trip, just that it's now even more obvious."

"It's called friendship."

"I've never noticed you look like that when you see me," Stephanie teased, coming around the desk to sit next to Julia. "Please tell me you aren't seriously going to make that gorgeous man wait until you graduate before you go out with him."

Julia sighed and went back to typing her note into the computer.

Stephanie leaned forward and tapped her hand in a light smack. "I'm serious. What if he gets tired of waiting and starts dating someone else? He's too awesome to risk losing to someone who won't make him wait months and months."

"His dating someone else would be okay." The pinching sensation in her chest hinted she might be wrong. "Honestly, I expect him to."

Stephanie gave her an odd look. "Are you hoping he does, Julia? Is that why you refuse to budge on your no-dating-until-graduation rule?"

"No. Maybe. I—I don't know," she answered truthfully. There was a part of her that was terrified of getting closer to Boone. Perhaps even their friendship was too much. She had no doubt it was going to sting something fierce when he bored of her. "It would be for the best in the long run if he did start dating someone else."

Stephanie gave her a horrified look. "Why would you think that?"

"We've nothing in common."

"I didn't get that impression in Gatlinburg. Y'all seemed to get along fabulously."

"That was one weekend." They had, but a weekend getaway wasn't the real world.

"Y'all get along just fine here at the hospital, too."

The hospital was the real world, but in a very isolated environment.

Julia arched a brow. "He's a great doctor. Why wouldn't I get along with him?"

"Exactly. Why wouldn't any sane woman get along with a charming, fun, considerate, smart, successful man like Boone? I know your reasons for wanting to keep school as your priority. I even admire your determination to achieve success and am so proud of you, Julia. But one of life's greatest gifts is that as new and exciting things happen, we can adjust how we define success. Doing well in life and school isn't exclusive of dating. You're a smart lady. I've no doubt that you can do both without compromising your commitment to yourself." Stephanie looked her directly in the eyes. "You wrote your Rules for Life Success. You can update them."

"I—maybe." For so long, she'd kept her focus on graduation, not allowing room for any diversion from the course she'd set. She was so close to the goal that changing paths now seemed an unnecessary risk. Why chance getting distracted with Boone? Already, he held way too much power over her. If she let him in...she'd be hurt.

"Maybe just go to dinner with Boone as friends, if nothing else," Stephanie encouraged her. "Spending Valentine's with him sure beats having your nose buried in the computer for schoolwork."

Except one was what she had planned and would help her achieve her long-term goals, and the other...the other...she just didn't know. She couldn't deny that she'd enjoyed their Gatlinburg trip. Nor could she say that he'd been anything short of wonderful since they'd returned. He'd been friendly, but she never felt he was pressuring her. Too bad she couldn't say the same for her inner voice. Stephanie was just vocalizing what her inner voice already whispered over and over, tempting her to explore her feelings for Boone.

Sighing, she glanced toward her best friend. "I repeat, Boone hasn't asked me to dinner for Valentine's."

"Not because he didn't want to," Boone said from the opposite end of the nurse station, obviously standing in her friend's field of vision. How long had he been there, and why hadn't Stephanie given Julia some warning?

As she turned toward him, taking in how handsome he looked in his light blue scrubs, Julia's face heated.

"Sorry." His eyes searched hers. "I came to tell you that I saw Aaron West in clinic and to let you know he's doing well. I didn't start out meaning to eavesdrop, but I couldn't help but overhear."

"I'm glad to hear Aaron is still doing well. As for the other, that's why having such conversations at work is a really bad idea."

"Or a really good one," her friend countered, flashing a big smile, then standing. "Sorry to rush off, but I need to check on my patient."

"Which could be interpreted as 'I'm off to leave the two of you alone,'" Julia accused her, but Stephanie just waved her fingers at Boone, then disappeared down the hallway.

"Forgive her. She can't help herself." Julia made light of the embarrassing conversation. Why hadn't she realized he was there? Of all times for her Boone awareness tingles to fail her...

"I like her," Boone said.

"I used to," Julia admitted with a soft smile. "Truly, I'm sorry for what she was saying."

"Because you don't want to have Valentine's dinner with me?"

Because I want to so desperately that I can barely keep from averting my gaze from yours.

"It would be better if we didn't."

"Having dinner alone doesn't sound as if it would be better," he pointed out, the corner of his mouth hiking up.

"I'm not asking you to be alone that night, just not to ask me." If he did spend it with someone else, she'd rather not know. Or maybe it would be best if she did so she could squash down the crazy notions he put into her mind.

His brows veed. "You want me to spend Valentine's with someone else?"

No. "If you did, then you wouldn't be alone for dinner on Valentine's."

He came around the desk and leaned against her workstation. "I'm of the opinion that being alone is preferable to being with the wrong person."

Her breath caught at what she saw in his eyes. "I'm not the right person."

He studied her for a long moment. Julia could barely breathe. "Maybe not," he finally said. "I look forward to when we can figure that out. Until then, what's Valentine's dinner between friends? No strings attached."

Her mind reeled from how his blue eyes were drawing her in. She wanted nothing more than to drown in their warmth. "Bad idea. Valentine's Day is meant for spending with lovers rather than friends."

For one moment she thought he was going to pounce on her comment. "We can start a new tradition. I would enjoy taking you to a Friends-lentine," his face twisted. "Friend-tine?" he tried again, then shook his head. "Val-friend-tine Day?"

He got an A for effort, but she shook her head. "Taking me to dinner on Valentine's sounds too much like a date."

"You could meet me at the restaurant and pay for your meal," he suggested as if that would resolve all her concerns.

She eyed him suspiciously. "You'd let me do that?"

"Not if I was on a date," he clarified. "But if that's the only way a friend would save me from a lonely evening—" he turned on the puppy-dog eyes "—then sure, why wouldn't I?"

The look he gave her was so over-the-top imploring that she couldn't hold in her laughter. "You should have gone into sales, Boone. Sorry, but I work on Valentine's."

"Me, too. But we both have to eat, so a late dinner works. I can book us reservations at—"

His excitement making her a little off balance, Julia interrupted. "Nowhere that requires reservations. That would be too date-like."

As if spending time on Valentine's with him wasn't going to feel that way already.

What had she done?

* * *

At around 3:00 p.m. on Valentine's Day, Julia blinked at her nurse director. "What do you mean I can go home?"

"Census is low. You know that with less patients admitted I have to send someone home, and today it's you." Patti waved her hands at Julia in a shooing motion. "Go. Before I change my mind."

Patti wasn't having it. "You always stay so someone else can go home or when we need someone to stay over. I'm not allowing it today. Quit arguing and get out of here."

"Do I even want to know why you chose today to insist I leave?" Was it possible that Stephanie had gotten to their boss? Not that her friend had control over the unit's census, but she wouldn't put it past Stephanie to have begged Patti to send Julia home early if the opportunity arose. Her friend had wanted to take her shopping for a new outfit and to have her hair done. Julia had declined, citing that she'd be spending her off-work day doing the studying she'd have otherwise done on Valentine's.

"Blame the census." Patti's grin said Julia should place blame on her, too. Did all her co-workers know she was having dinner with Boone? Although no one had directly asked, she'd gotten a lot of knowing smiles since New

Year's. Several of their work group at been there, had seen them, so it was no secret they'd spent time together there. Still…

The truth was, Julia would rather work late than go home early. Working late meant not obsessing about getting ready for a Valentine's dinner that wasn't a date, yet she had bees buzzing around in her belly. She'd refused Stephanie's offer, but that didn't mean she hadn't thought about what she would wear. She'd gone through her closet a dozen times, pulling out one outfit, then another. Everything seemed either too dressy or too casual.

After asking her about her food likes and dislikes, Boone had texted her an address for a mom-and-pop restaurant near downtown and promised they'd have a low-stress, no-pressure evening where they could relax—as friends. She settled on a bright red sweater, a pair of black jeans, boots, and silver hoop earrings and a bangle bracelet. She'd just finished brushing her hair when her phone rang. Seeing Boone's number, her heart thudded.

"There's been a change of plans."

Julia winced. He was canceling. She took a deep breath. This was for the best. She knew it was. "No problem. I have a ton to do anyway, and—"

"You think I'm canceling? That's not the

change of plans, Julia. The only thing that's changed is where you're driving to."

That she felt such relief at his words should have had her running.

"I think you'll enjoy this better than the restaurant I originally chose. I'll text you the address and see you in about fifteen minutes, if that works?"

Excitement laced his voice. Excitement that hinted she hadn't been alone in stressed anticipation of the evening. Excitement that had her curious. Just a dinner between friends…who was she kidding? Dinner with a friend had never had her feeling so…so…aware of every beat of her heart.

If she wasn't careful, it was the breaking of her heart that she was going to be so aware of.

CHAPTER SEVEN

HOPING HE HADN'T made a major miscalculation, Boone glanced around his kitchen for his and Julia's Valentine's plans. Going to a restaurant where they'd be surrounded by amorous couples had seemed more high-pressure, though. His hope was to keep tonight light and fun, and for Julia to relax the way she had in Gatlinburg. He got glimpses of that woman at the hospital, but whether it was her way of clinging to professionalism or just to keep space between them, she fought giving him those glimpses.

When she did, those smiles melted his insides and had him craving more. Which was the story of his relationship with Julia—him craving more.

His phone rang. Seeing her number, he answered, "You're not allowed to cancel."

"Ha. That's what I thought you were doing when you called earlier." He could hear her smile, and giddiness filled him. "But perhaps unfortunately for you, I'm not calling to cancel.

Although maybe I should. I'm confused. I'm sitting in the driveway of a fancy house in a fancy subdivision rather than in a restaurant parking lot." She paused. "Why is that?"

She was there.

"Have you ever heard of one of those places where you prepare your meal, then eat it?" he asked, heading toward the front door. "This is one of those."

"I'm cooking my meal at someone's house?"

"We're cooking our dinner together. It'll be fun." Worried that she might drive away, Boone opened his front door, smiling at the image of her sitting in the driver's seat of her small sedan. After a moment's hesitation, she got out of her car and headed toward him. She'd left her hair loose, and it spilled from beneath the stretchy red hat with a fuzzy ball on top that matched her gloves and scarf. Seeing her wearing the gifts he'd given her to replace the scarf he'd used at Ober, he smiled. Was she also wearing his necklace? He'd swear he caught glimpses of the chain from time to time, but she kept the pendant tucked beneath her clothes. Anticipation built in him with every step she took toward him. Tonight was going to be a good night. A great night. He'd keep things simple just as she'd asked. They'd have good food and relax with no one around except the two of them. No pressure.

When she joined him on the porch stoop, she arched a brow. "Why don't you have on shoes?"

Glancing down at his bare feet poking out from the bottom of his jeans, the cold of the porch registering for the first time, he shrugged. "It's a casual night between friends. I didn't think shoes were necessary. You're welcome to take off your shoes, too, but I recommend waiting until we're inside because you forgot your bear blanket to warm you up."

Looking as if she might take flight, she eyed him. "This is your house, isn't it?"

"Is that a problem?" He stepped aside for her to come in.

"It's not good." Rather than turn around and leave, she entered, glancing around his foyer in a way that had him doing the same, trying to see the interior-decorator-designed room through Julia's eyes. He liked the clean, crisp white lines of his home. It was functional and a place where he could relax.

"Sure it is. Just think, you don't have to worry about anyone seeing us and making false assumptions that we're anything more than friends."

"It's been too late for that ever since we got back from Gatlinburg. Perhaps even the Christmas party. I'm sure that's how I ended up being sent home early due to low census today." Julia played with the end of the red scarf wrapped around her neck. "My being at your house isn't a good idea, Boone. I should go."

"Please don't, Julia. I give you my word that I didn't invite you here for nefarious reasons. Tonight is dinner made together by friends and us relaxing without any outside pressure of being surrounded by couples prone to PDA because of the holiday. Please stay."

Looking torn, she took a deep breath, then another. Her chest rose and fell beneath her puffy black jacket. Then she sighed. "Why do I think I'm going to regret this?"

"This is good," Julia admitted later that night, taking another bite of the pizza she and Boone had made together. He'd had all their supplies out, giving her options to create whatever kind of pizza she wanted. He'd bought a couple of different premade crusts, and they'd rolled out the one she'd picked onto a round baking stone, then piled on various toppings. Once they had it baking in the oven, they'd made salads and ate them while the pizza filled his house with its delicious scent.

He grinned. "You doubted me when I told you it would be?"

"Not really," she admitted, taking another bite of the cheesy goodness. "Short of burning, it's difficult to mess up pizza."

"Our salad was pretty good, too," he reminded her. He sat catty-corner to her at the large black-granite-topped island in the pristine white kitchen. The kitchen was the nicest she'd ever been in. She'd felt awkward as if she hadn't belonged, but he'd been so relaxed having her there that it had been difficult to think of anything other than his smile and teasing as they prepared their meal.

"Salads are also difficult to mess up," she pointed out, holding up a half-eaten pizza slice. "The real test is whatever you have planned for dessert."

His lips twitched. "Who said anything about dessert?"

"No dessert?" She tsked, then tossed some pepperoni at him. "There went our friendship. Did you learn nothing about me in Gatlinburg? Dessert is my favorite part of a meal."

Eyes sparkling, he caught the pepperoni. "Seems like I did notice that you have a sweet tooth. I'll have to come up with something. Can't have our friendship ending over sweets." He popped the pepperoni into his mouth. "Let's finish our pizza, watch television while our food settles, and then we'll see about dessert."

"So, you do have something sweet planned?"

He grinned. "Was there ever any doubt?"

That he wouldn't provide the most perfect

evening? Not really. She suspected everything Boone set his mind to went off without a hitch. He was that kind of guy, and if this had been a dinner date, she'd admit, it would have been an absolutely perfect one.

Good thing it wasn't.

Boone glanced at Julia hugging a pillow to her. He'd agonized over what entertainment to have on tap for their evening, debating a romantic comedy versus an action thriller versus something else. What type of show said "we're just two friends watching a movie together"? What type of show said that without really sliding him into a just-friends zone? Because he didn't want to get stuck there.

He'd forgone movies altogether since Julia would have to drive herself home late. He'd chosen a family rivalry game show with a host sure to elicit laughter. Laughter was good. He wanted Julia to smile and laugh. Just as she was doing that very moment. Unlike when she'd first walked into his house, she'd relaxed and had even kicked off her shoes.

Sensing that he was watching her rather than the show, she cut her gaze toward him and brushed her fingers over her lips. "What? Do I have sauce on my face or something?"

"No sauce. I was just admiring that you're enjoying yourself."

"Top one hundred survey says...you're right. I am. Thank you for dinner, even if I had to help prepare it myself." Her smile said she hadn't minded. "I'm still curious about dessert."

At her mention of sweets again, he grinned. "We'll finish watching this episode to see if they win the money. Then we'll see what we can rustle up."

"I have to help cook that, too?" She gave an exaggerated sigh.

"You'll see." He started to tell her that someday, when they were dating, he'd cook for her. Tonight, he didn't want to risk ruining their evening by mentioning anything about the future. For now, having her here was enough. It had to be since she wasn't giving him a choice.

Watching the show, they each called out their answers as the host asked the questions, laughing when they gave three of five answers exactly the same.

"Great minds," he mused.

The episode ended with the family getting the necessary points to win the money.

"Yay! They won."

"Because they gave the same answers you did," he pointed out. "Four of five of your answers were the number one pick. You should apply to be on the show."

Her face flashed pale for the briefest second. Then she shook her head. "It's a family show, Boone. I don't have five family members."

Boone cringed. He'd made the comment without thought. He knew bits and pieces of her background and hadn't gotten the impression that she was close to her family, but he hadn't realized that was because there was no family. "No aunts or uncles? No cousins?"

She shook her head. "There's just me and my dad. It's possible he has more children, but none that he's ever mentioned. Last I spoke with him there was another stepmother as well, but I haven't talked with him for a while, so that may have changed."

"He doesn't live around here?"

She shrugged. "If he did, it wouldn't be for long. He's always on the move with one job or another. He works construction and goes wherever the next job is. We've never been close."

She was such a kind, big-hearted person that it was difficult to imagine her not being close to her one remaining relative. He would have guessed she'd have clung to that relationship. That she didn't said a lot about the man who'd played a role in her existence. The guy must be a real loser.

"What happened to your mother?"

"She died." For a moment he thought he'd messed up, that she was going to clam up and find a reason to leave. Instead, she took a deep breath. "My family doesn't make for great Valentine's dinner conversation. What about you? You've mentioned parents and a brother. You're a smart guy, so if they're anything like you, then maybe you should audition for the show."

There had been a sister, as well. A beautiful, brilliant twin sister who had gotten involved with the wrong crowd and ended up taking her life, whether by accident or intentionally, by overdosing on a mixture of too many pills and too much alcohol. His heart ached with the void left at her death. A part of him had died that day. He'd known before he'd gotten the call that something was wrong, that she was gone, and he'd tried to reach her to no avail. He'd… No, he couldn't let his thoughts go down that rabbit hole. He refocused on his conversation with Julia and shook his head.

"It would never work with my family. A feud would break out, for sure. We'd all want to be in charge."

Curiosity shone on her face. "Who would win?"

"My mother," he answered without hesitation, smiling as her face flashed through his mind.

He'd run his Valentine's dinner plan by her, and she'd given her approval. She'd also been curious about the woman who he kept talking about, but who was keeping him at arm's length. Part of him wouldn't have been surprised if she'd arrived in time for dinner so she could meet Julia. He loved that overall, she seemed to be doing well these days. For so long after Amy's death, she hadn't.

"I guess she had to be tough to be the only female in the house."

She hadn't been the only one. But just as Julia hadn't wanted to talk about her mother, he really didn't want to kill the vibe between them by telling her how his twin sister had chosen drugs over life. Amy was heavy conversation, just as he knew Julia's mother was. He suspected they had a lot in common in that regard. "Mom is definitely tough. Come on. Let's eat dessert. I won't even make you do the prep work."

She eyed him as if she knew there was something he hadn't said, but after a moment she smiled. "What? I don't have to work for dessert?"

"You'll be excited to hear that I did take note of your appreciation of sweeter things and stopped by that shop just down from the hospital. I may have gone a little overboard." He opened the pantry and pulled out the goodies he'd hidden away.

Her jaw dropped. "Oh, wow. We'll never eat all that."

"We can have fun trying," he suggested. "You get first pick."

She eyed the platter that held everything from chocolate-covered strawberries to cupcakes. "This is insane. I don't want to know what this cost."

"To see that light in your eyes, I consider every penny paid a bargain."

She frowned. "Stop it with the smarmy lines."

He could argue that he'd told her the truth, but instead put the platter onto the counter. "Which do you want to try first?"

"They all look good," she mused, studying the offering. "Let's share and sample several of them." She picked a white-chocolate-covered strawberry and took a bite, catching part of the candy coating that came loose. "Oh, this is heaven."

Watching her was heaven. Or maybe that other place, because he'd broken a sweat. Friends, he reminded himself. Tonight was just two friends having dinner. Friends to lovers, he thought. Because someday Julia would admit to the attraction between them. Until then he'd play by her rules because the end prize would be worth it. Despite his frustration, he admired her dedication to obtaining her degree and having a better life than the one she'd had.

"Taste?" she asked, holding the berry toward him.

Rather than taking the berry from her, he leaned in and, gaze locked with hers, bit into the candy-coated fruit she held. She was right. It was good. But not nearly as good as what he saw in her eyes. There was a promise there. A promise of things to come that was undeniable no matter how much she'd fought it.

She finished the berry, chose a truffle, then flashed a bright smile his way. "Best Val-friends-tine dessert ever. Thank you."

"You're welcome, *friend*."

She was his friend.

She was also so much more.

"I need a favor," Boone announced six weeks later.

Trying to tamp down her awareness tingles, Julia glanced up from the medicine cart. As always, her breath caught at the sight of him. Wearing navy scrubs embroidered with his name, his stethoscope poking out of his pocket, and a smile on his handsome face, he looked like he should star on a television show. She'd sure tune in each episode.

"I'll help if I can."

"Great. Go to Memphis with me next weekend."

"What?" She'd been expecting him to ask her to round on a patient with him or to help with a procedure, not go out of town with him. Things had been good between them since Valentine's Day. He'd been friendly, sought her company at work, but hadn't pushed to spend time with her outside of the hospital, for which she'd been grateful because of her school workload. He had to know she wouldn't agree to go out of town with him, especially not to his hometown. "That's a mighty big favor. Before I say no, do you want to tell me why you need me to go?"

"I'll tell you, but not so that you can say no." He looked straight into her eyes. "It's my birthday. My parents are throwing a party."

"Then I definitely shouldn't go with you." She couldn't believe he wanted her to go, but even if the timing was right, she knew his family was well-to-do, that they were very close, and that any woman, friend or otherwise, that he brought home would be under great scrutiny. No, thank you.

"There will be cake," he said as if that would tilt the scales in his favor. After the way they'd pigged out on Valentine's, she could see why he might think that, but there wasn't enough sugar on the planet to convince her to say yes. However, there was something in his eyes that called to her, a sadness that seemed at odds with his teasing comment.

"Tempting, but no." What was with his eyes? With her sense that there was something deeper to his request? She scratched at a stray piece of tape on the cart. "Going out of town right now doesn't work. My thesis is due in two weeks. I have just over a month before graduation."

"Knowing you, your thesis is done and you're just fine-tuning your wording, obsessing over making sure it's perfect before you turn it in. I could help with that, read over it for you, make suggestions, look for weak spots, point out how amazing it is." He put his hand on her arm, his thumb grazing over her tattoo and sending zings through her. "I know I'm asking a lot, but please go, Julia. This may sound crazy, but I need you there."

Breath catching, she glanced up, meeting his eyes again. Big mistake, because she'd swear he really did need her to be there with him, which was highly confusing as she knew he got along great with his family. Why would he need her there? Torn, she bit her lower lip and dropped her hand from the cart so his would naturally fall away. She couldn't think clearly with him touching her.

"On top of everything else, my brother's bring-

ing his girlfriend's single and interested sister."
He wrinkled his nose. "She's excited to meet me
and wants to know if I have a favorite dinner-
ware pattern."

Was he trying to convince her to run interfer-
ence or to make her jealous? She'd be the first
to tell him he should meet this woman. Well,
maybe. Glancing away, she mumbled, "Lucky
you."

"You think? If you don't go, I'll be avoiding
matchmaking all weekend."

"She may be great."

"That doesn't matter when she's not you."

At his words, Julia's knees almost buckled,
and she grabbed hold of the medicine cart to
steady herself on the spinning tile floor. Did he
have any idea how what he was saying sounded?
How much their growing closeness scared her?

"It's not uncommon for someone to bring a
friend to a birthday party," he continued.

"A friend who's the opposite sex?"

"I don't discriminate based upon gender." He
gave her a hopeful look. "Going home alone for
one's birthday is no fun, you know?"

She'd never gone home for her birthday, so she
didn't know. What would have been the point?
Birthdays had never been big deals even when
her mother had been alive. Whether or not her

mother would acknowledge the day was always a fifty-fifty toss-up.

"Friends don't let friends go home alone." His tone teased, but his eyes still held the hint of sorrow that had her insides knotting. "I'd owe you big time."

She should say no. She knew she should. No it was. Then she was walking away.

"Okay, I'll go." That's not what she'd meant to say. Traitorous tongue. "But only if Mrs. Smithfield can watch Honey."

"Thank you, Julia." A smile spread across his face. "You're not going to regret this."

Part of her already did. What was she doing? Going with Boone was nothing short of masochistic. Pure craziness.

The following weekend, sitting in the passenger seat of Boone's car, she was still telling herself the same thing. Her thesis truly had already been written. He'd read it the previous weekend and given her a few suggestions for tweaks, but that was it. She'd made the changes and read it to him during the first part of their drive.

"The changes are perfect," he assured her.

"I thought so, too. Thank you for suggesting them."

She pulled out study cards for her certification exam scheduled for after graduation.

Boone had her read the questions out loud,

give an answer, and then they'd discuss what the book had as the correct answer. Not a quick way to study, but she was unlikely to forget any of the items they touched on during their drive.

Keeping his gaze on the interstate, he asked, "How does it feel to know that you essentially have a month left of school?"

"Assuming that I don't opt to get my doctorate," she mused, pulling out a fresh stack of question cards from the book bag in the car's floorboard.

He briefly looked toward her. "You're smart enough that if it's something you want to do, then you should. You can do anything you set your mind to."

"Except say no to you?" The teasing question slipped out, but warmth spread through her chest at his words. She was able to do anything she set her mind to. No one had ever believed in her that way. That Boone truly did… Her eyes prickled with moisture that she refused to let escape.

He chuckled. "You're an expert at telling me no."

"Just not with sticking to it," she mumbled, glancing out the passenger window. The sun had started its descent and streaked the sky with orange hues, highlighting Nashville's skyline as they moved through the city marking their halfway point.

"Why does hearing you say that make me feel as if I'm a bad guy for convincing you to go with me this weekend? My goal is for you to want to say yes, Julia, not for you to feel you've conceded defeat when we spend time together."

"It's never been a matter of me not wanting to say yes to you, Boone," she admitted, clenching the note cards.

"It must be my birthday, because that's the nicest thing you've ever said to me."

Julia snorted. "Tomorrow is your birthday, and I'm always nice to you."

"True." Nodding, he tapped his fingers against the steering wheel to some beat only he heard as they'd had the radio off while reviewing her questions. "But I appreciate what you said, Julia. It gives me hope that you won't change your mind about celebrating your graduation with me."

She stared at him a bit in awe. He was serious. It was the end of March. He was still singing the same song, that he wanted to date her, that she was worth waiting for. Rather than changing his mind, he was concerned she was the one who wouldn't go. "I just don't understand you. Why are you doing this?"

His gaze flicked toward her, then quickly returned to the road. "This?"

"Waiting months for my graduation to take me on a date when you could be dating any number of women, Boone. I'm not oblivious to the fact that other women want you."

"That makes one of us, then, because I haven't noticed, other than my brother threatening me with Leslie's sister. But even if I had noticed, it doesn't matter what other women want. You're the woman in my life, as my friend until you're agreeable to something more."

She was the woman in his life. Whether she insisted upon calling it friendship until after a calendar date, he had been faithful to his claim that he'd wait. That he had boggled her mind.

"Did you have many girlfriends prior to Dr. Cunningham?"

He shrugged. "A few during high school and university. None that lasted as long as my relationship with Olivia, though."

"Do you still talk to her?" That wasn't jealousy coursing through her body. Maybe.

"Occasionally, but she hasn't forgiven me yet. She's gone out with one of her coworkers a few times and has realized what I already had—that she and I weren't in love."

Julia let what he said sink in. "You believe love exists?"

"Don't you?"

Did she? "It's not something I've had much experience with or even thought about much."

"No past boyfriends who stole your heart?"

"None worth talking about." Most of the men in her life had been the result of being intoxicated and not knowing or caring what she was doing. With Clay, she'd been clean, on track with her Rules for Life Success, and thought she'd found someone who saw beyond her past.

"Is it wrong for me to say that I'm glad?" He shot her a sheepish grin. "It's admittedly selfish of me, but I'd like to be the first."

Heat flooded through her. What was he saying?

"I'm not a virgin, Boone." She shoved the question cards back into their box and pushed them into the book bag. "If that's what you're referring to, then just get over yourself, because I doubt you are, either."

"Calm down. I wasn't referring to sex. Nor did I intend to make you so defensive. But my statement is still true." He paused, then said, "I meant that if you're going to fall in love, I'd like it to be with me."

She'd been nervously rummaging through her bag to pull out a study guide. Now her breath caught. She straightened and gawked at him. "That would be a horrible thing for me to do. You'd break my heart."

"I'm more concerned that you're going to break mine."

Heartbeat pounding in her ears, Julia glanced

down at the book in her lap. The words blurred until she couldn't read them. No matter. Her focus was completely shot, anyway.

It would be so easy to give in to the sweetness of Boone's words. But not in a million years did she believe he'd be the one left with a broken heart.

They drove in silence. Julia pretended to study as she absently toyed with the pendant he'd given her, the diamond a stark reminder of their economic differences. Who knew what Boone was thinking?

What had possessed her to say yes to going with him this weekend? She wouldn't fit into his world. She knew that. Had she needed to see proof? A visible reminder of why she needed to say no and stick to it?

She had less than a month until graduation. Then what?

You have to tell him everything and let him decide if he wants to spend time with someone who was once very broken and sometimes still feels barely held together. And if he does, you have to be prepared that he'll change his mind and end up leaving, anyway.

CHAPTER EIGHT

EVEN BEFORE THEY arrived in Memphis, Boone sensed how uncomfortable Julia was, but from the moment they'd pulled through the gated entrance to his parents' home, she'd clammed up. Or maybe that had happened when he'd said things aloud that he shouldn't even be thinking, much less giving voice to. The words had just slipped out. Words that needed to slip out were to tell her about Amy. He missed her, but tomorrow would be harder than most days. How could it not when he'd spent most of his life sharing birthday celebrations with her?

They arrived around ten. Introductions had been made, polite but guarded on Julia's part, pleasantries exchanged. His father, an older version of Boone minus the blue eyes he'd inherited from his mother, wore a tie and slacks, and his mother looked elegant in a slim A-line dress that hinted they'd been out for dinner. They looked happy, which did Boone's heart good, because for a long time there hadn't been many smiles. He and Julia visited with them for about half an hour. Then his mother had shown Julia to a guest room. He'd texted her good-night, but she'd not responded until that morning, when she'd asked what time she needed to be downstairs.

He'd met her at the bottom of the stairs, admiring her brightly patterned top, relaxed jeans, and sandals. She'd left her hair long about her shoulders, but he noted the band around her wrist in case she opted to pull it back later in the day.

Rather than a more intimate family meal at the breakfast nook, his mother had pulled out all the stops. They were in the large formal dining room with their longtime housekeeper, Sue Ellen, serving the meal. Justin, his girlfriend Leslie, and her sister Jacqueline were there, along with his parents, one of his dad's two brothers and his wife, and two cousins and their significant others. Excited to finally meet the woman he'd been talking about for months, his mother was dressed to a tee in black slacks and a button-down blouse. She zeroed in on Julia, wanting to know as much about her as she could. Add in everyone else's curiosity and Julia was facing nonstop questions, and it wasn't even 8:00 a.m. yet. No wonder she kept rubbing her tattoo as if it gave her magical powers to face whatever his family tossed at her.

His mother smiled at Julia between sips of her

straight black coffee. "Have you visited Memphis before, Julia?"

Pausing with her fork midair, Julia shook her head. "No, ma'am. My parents moved a lot when I was small, so it's possible, but I don't think so."

"Your parents live in Knoxville now?"

Julia shook her head. "My mother passed when I was seventeen, and my father lives wherever his current construction job is located."

His mother reached for her toast, the light catching the large diamond on her finger that his father had given her for their thirtieth anniversary a few years back. "We look forward to meeting him. You'll have to let him know that he should reach out if his work brings him to Memphis. We could meet for lunch."

Julia's gaze bounced from his mother's ring to Boone. Regret in coming was etched in her brown eyes. He'd been so blinded by his desire to have her there, to not go home alone for a party he'd rather not have, that he hadn't considered just how much his parents would overwhelm her. He wanted her meeting his family to be positive, not an uptight torture session. That weekend probably wasn't the best choice.

She fielded more questions, politely, and always with a smile that he recognized as forced. He interjected frequently, asking his dad or brother about their work, asking his mom about the shipping business, but his mother repeatedly came back to Julia.

"Julia, Robert and I have a quick errand, but afterwards, you'll have to join me in making sure the last-minute details of Boone's birthday bash are perfect while the others play golf this morning."

Not that Julia couldn't hold her own, but Boone wasn't leaving her at his mother's mercy. "Sorry, Mom, but Julia can't visit Memphis without seeing Graceland."

His mother's brow arched. "You're not going with the others?"

"Not unless Julia prefers golf to my corny Elvis impressions." He turned to Julia, willed her to meet his gaze, and was relieved when she did. "What do you think? We can slip away for a few hours, see Graceland, have lunch on Mud Island or Beale Street, and still be back in plenty of time to get ready for the party."

Forever polite, Julia glanced toward his mother. "If there's something you need, I'd be happy to help."

For a moment Boone thought his mother was going to suggest Julia stay. His father must have too, because he spoke up. "If Boone wants to show you his hometown, then that's fine, isn't it, dear?" He gave his wife a look that said she should agree. "We wouldn't want to put our son's guest to work the first time she visits our home."

Although Boone knew she wasn't happy about having her time alone with Julia foiled, his mother, ever the perfect hostess, conceded. "Of course Julia should go with Boone. I never would have suggested she stay if I'd realized Boone hadn't planned to play golf." She reached over and patted Boone's hand. "I'd thought she and I would have girl time while the rest of you did your thing."

"Maybe some other time, but Julia's mine for the day."

After visiting with his family and finishing their meal, Boone whisked Julia from the house.

"Sorry about that," he said the moment they were outside the house. "Are you an Elvis fan?"

Following him to his car in the circle drive in front of the house, Julia shrugged. "I know some of his songs."

Which wasn't a glowing review of his suggestion. "We don't have to go if you don't want to. Mom is a huge Elvis fan, so it's what first popped into my mind."

"It's fine. I've never been. Sorry. I'm still processing everything from this morning."

Before the day was over, she'd have a lot more to process. His stomach clenched at the thought of telling her about his sister, but he needed to prior to the party tonight. Someone might mention Amy, and he didn't want Julia blindsided. Still, he'd wait until later in the day.

They toured Graceland. Julia finally relaxed about midway through the tour, laughing at his Elvis impersonations and reminding him not to quit his day job.

"Your family's home is more impressive," she pointed out as they ended at the site where Elvis and his parents were buried on the property. "You could sell tours."

"We don't have a room full of gold albums." He reached for her hand and was grateful when she didn't pull away. "Come on. We'll drive down by the Pyramid. Mud Island is right next to it and we'll have an early lunch there and walk along the river."

"Oh wow. It really is a pyramid," Julia said, staring out the window at the shiny structure.

"It really is. It was once called the Great American Pyramid and was an arena, but now it's owned by a sporting goods store that takes up the first few floors. Higher up is a hotel and at the top there's a bar with an observation deck. We can go there after lunch if you'd like."

"Maybe." But her gaze had gone to the Mississippi River.

"It's really muddy, isn't it?" she said of the brown water separating Tennessee from Arkansas.

"I've never seen it that it wasn't." He drove them to a trendy, low-key café with a river view.

"I can't believe I just ate all that after such a huge breakfast." Julia patted her belly. "If I don't slow down, I won't fit into my dress for tonight."

He ran his gaze over her, liking what he saw. A lot. "I'm glad you're enjoying yourself."

"It's hard not to enjoy oneself when something is as delicious as what we just ate." She glanced at her watch. "Do we still have time to walk? I'd love to stretch my legs."

Boone nodded. "Do you want to walk by the river or along the neighborhood here? There's several interesting stores in the area if you'd like to do some shopping."

"I may need to do both." Laughing, she patted her stomach again. "But by the river would be great."

They crossed the street to walk along the sidewalk than ran beside the Mississippi River with the Hernando de Soto Bridge to their backs. Boone reached for her hand and was filled with happiness when her fingers clasped his.

The breeze coming off the river whipped at her hair. "Thank you for my Memphis mini-tour and for lunch. It's been nice."

"You weren't expecting it to be?"

Glancing out toward a barge floating down the river, she shrugged. "I wasn't prepared for how big your parents' home was. I've never known anyone who lived on an estate."

Trying to make sure he chose his words wisely as he didn't want to make light or too big a deal of his family's success, he waited until a bicycler had ridden past.

"I lived there most of my life. It was my grandparents' home. Mom grew up there. When she and Dad married, she wanted to stay, so they did. I never thought much about us living with my grandparents. I didn't realize it wasn't common for families to do so until my early teenage years."

"It's big enough for several families. I've never known someone with a live-in housekeeper, either."

"Sue Ellen and her husband originally worked for my grandparents. As you said, it's a big place. Mom and Dad have busy lives. It made sense to keep them on after my grandfather passed. They're like extended family."

She gave him a get-serious look. "Extended family who serves you breakfast and cleans up after you?"

"It's what they are paid to do, just as my father is paid to provide medical care and Mom to run the shipping company. As with most families, different members carry different roles. My parents take very good care of them and vice versa. Does that bother you?"

Continuing to walk, she stared out toward the muddy river. "Not really. It's just yet another example of how different our lives are."

"Differences can complement each other," he reminded her.

"Or pull in opposite directions."

He gave her hand a gentle squeeze. "We have more in common than you think."

"What exactly is it that we have in common?"

"We'll start with the obvious things like that we both live in Knoxville, work at the same hospital, and want to take good care of our patients. We both enjoy dessert and have a thing for fuzzy bear blankets."

She snorted. "With all that, how could I have ever doubted our similarities?"

"I know, right?" He grinned. "Plus, there's this." He lifted their entwined hands and pressed a kiss to her fingers.

She turned to him, the breeze making her hair dance about her face. The sunlight gilded the brunette strands. "What's that exactly?"

"You don't feel that flutter in your stomach the way I do when we touch? Maybe I'm wrong, but I'd swear you do, Julia. Your heart races just as mine does, and that's why you came with me this weekend."

She swallowed. "I came because it's your birthday."

"And because you care about me," he pressed.

"Of course, I care about you. We're coworkers."

Boone had been patient for months, knew he needed to continue to be patient, that if he pushed too hard, Julia might forever shut him out. Perhaps it was because they were so far away from Knoxville, or that he was on his home turf, but rather than back down, he stared into her eyes and asked, "That's all I am to you? A coworker?"

Surprise darkened her eyes. "We agreed to be friends."

Which was a sharp reminder that he shouldn't be pressing.

"True. We did. Is that all you see us ever being?"

"What is it you want me to say, Boone? That I see us going from friends to lovers after I graduate? Is it that you want me to admit that my trying to keep us as just friends is a miserable failure?"

Even as he felt shame for pressing, Boone's chest puffed at what she'd admitted with her questions. "I've not tried to hide my feelings from you. You know what I want, Julia."

She sighed. "I just don't understand why me."

"Why you?" Unable to resist, he brushed a flyaway hair behind her ear, tucking it back. The touch wasn't enough, and he cupped her face. "Because you are a good person. You're kind, a fantastic nurse and friend. Your smile lights up any room, and the feel of your skin against mine makes me aware of every nerve ending in my body."

She took a sharp intake of breath but didn't pull away.

"You're beautiful on the inside and out," he continued. "When I'm with you, the world takes on a sharper edge, as if life is somehow more in focus, more vivid in color."

"You don't know what you're saying." Her eyes closed, but she didn't pull away. Instead, she nuzzled her cheek against where he held her.

"You're wrong, Julia. I know exactly what I'm saying, what I'm feeling. We can call it friendship for however long you insist, but what's happening between us is more."

"I don't like it," she admitted, squeezing her eyes more tightly. "It scares me. You scare me."

He bent and kissed the top of her head, inhaling the vanilla fragrance he would forever associate with her. "Don't be afraid, Julia. Not of me."

"You just don't know," she began, shaking her head, then looking up. When she did so, her face was so close to his that he could feel her breath as it mingled with his own and completely intoxicated his better judgment.

His gaze dropped to her mouth, and he longed for his lips to touch hers, softly, just for a quick taste. Only, a quick taste of her mouth wouldn't be enough. All he really wanted was to pull her to him, devour her mouth, devour her body, and lose himself with her until they could no longer tell where the one ended and the other started. He lifted his gaze to hers.

What he saw swirling in the brown depths of her eyes dissolved what little willpower remained. Because shining there was longing for all the same things.

Stunned, Julia stared up at the man who had just said the sweetest things to her. Never in her life had she been praised the way Boone did. But it was the sincerity with which he said them that unwound her best intentions. Boone meant what he was saying. Wonderful, brilliant Boone wanted her and thought she was amazing.

When his head lowered to close the short distance between their mouths, she didn't stop him, couldn't have if she'd wanted to, even though they were on a public sidewalk along the Mississippi. She hadn't wanted to. What she wanted was to feel Boone's lips against hers, to have him kiss her until she was breathless and too weak to resist. She wanted him.

But just as his lips would have claimed hers,

he turned his head, and rested his forehead against hers.

"One month, Julia. As much as I want to kiss you, I won't be the cause of you breaking the promise you made to yourself and have kept all this time. When we finally kiss—and make no mistake about it, we will—I don't want you to have regrets. If I kissed you now, you'd overflow with them." He brushed his fingertips across her cheek. "Just know, doing the right thing isn't easy."

Julia trembled at his gentle touch.

"Thank you," she managed, knowing he was right. As much as she longed to feel his lips against hers, she would beat herself up over her weakness where he was concerned. Not to mention there were people out enjoying the early spring sunshine and they'd have no privacy.

Not sure what else to say, she resumed their walk along the Mississippi. She'd never believed he'd stick around until her graduation. The thought of losing the way he looked at her, the way he touched her as if she was something exquisite, was enough to fill her with great sorrow. She should never have let herself get close to him.

She shouldn't have done a lot of things.

Falling for Boone Richards was at the top of the list.

* * *

Boone couldn't win for losing. He'd have regretted kissing her as he knew doing so prior to her graduation would bother her, yet he grieved what he could have had. In the moment, she'd not only been willing, she'd wanted his kiss.

After their almost-kiss, she suggested they head toward the shops, saying she should pick up a souvenir for Stephanie and, if anything, being overly bubbly to hide the underlying sexual tension that zapped between them.

"What do you think of this?" she asked, holding up an Elvis statue. "Does this scream Stephanie or what?"

Boone started to respond, but a fairy mixed in with the plethora of touristy items caught his eye. Someone had put the item on the wrong shelf as it didn't fit amidst the various iconic Memphis baubles. Barely able to breathe, he couldn't drag his eyes from the fairy.

Noticing, Julia asked, "You have a thing for fairies?"

"No, but Amy did."

Julia's expression softened. "You've mentioned her before, but not really told me who she was."

Boone picked up the fairy and traced over a wing. "Amy was my twin sister."

"Oh," Julia gasped. "I didn't realize…you had a twin?"

He nodded. "She overdosed my senior year of undergrad."

"I'm so sorry."

"Just something else we have in common." At Julia's pale face, he continued. "My sister and your mother died the same way."

"Oh. Yes. You're right." She seemed to struggle to get her thoughts together. "Today is her birthday, too, then?"

He nodded.

She gestured toward the fairy he held. "Maybe you should buy that for her."

"Huh?"

"You're looking at me as if I'm crazy. I… I just thought that since she liked fairies, maybe you could give her that as a birthday present." As he continued to stare at her, she grimaced. "I mean, if she's buried close by, that is."

Go to Amy's grave. He'd not been since the day he'd said his goodbyes. What was the point? She wasn't there. Not really. He went to put the fairy back on the shelf, but at the last moment, changed his mind.

"We could do that."

After Julia had paid for the Elvis and a T-shirt for Stephanie, he paid for the fairy, and they left the shop. Stepping outside the air-conditioned store and into the sunny day's heat had sweat popping out over his skin. That was the reason, and not the thought of going to the cemetery.

"Did Amy have a favorite flower?" Julia asked, gesturing to the florist next to the shop. "We could get some flowers to put on her grave."

Boone's throat tightened, but he managed to croak out, "Daisies. She liked daisies."

Heart aching, Julia clung to Boone's hand as they crossed the cemetery toward where his sister was buried. Amy had overdosed close to the time Julia herself had. She needed to tell him, but she'd never seen him distraught, and that was the only way she could describe him.

"I've never been back here," he said beside her, his palm clammy, as they reached the tombstone engraved with his sister's name. "I can't believe I'm here today, with you."

"I'm sorry if I shouldn't have suggested we come here."

Inhaling sharply, he shook his head. "I should have come years ago. Instead, I've just tried to forget. Just as the rest of my family avoids saying her name like she never existed because remembering is too painful."

Tears rolled down Julia's cheeks. "I'm sorry."

"Me, too. I should have been there for her. I didn't realize she'd started using again. I was in school, but how could I have missed that? She was my twin. We shared a special bond. I should have known."

"I'm sure she knew you loved her, Boone."

"It wasn't enough. I wasn't enough to keep her clean."

"You know addiction doesn't work that way."

Sighing, he stooped and placed the fairy and daisies on the grave, next to a huge arrangement that was a mixture of daisies and other spring flowers. "Mom and Dad must pay the grounds-keeper to tend to her grave."

"You don't think they were here? That this is the errand your mother mentioned?"

His face ashen, Boone's gaze cut to hers. "You think?"

Julia looked at the arrangement, at the care that had been taken, noting the slight impression on the grave as if someone had knelt there earlier. "I may be wrong, but that would be my guess."

To her surprise, and not letting go of her hand, Boone knelt in almost the same place that Julia suspected his parents had earlier in the day. She didn't comment on his tears, nor did he comment on hers.

When he stood and they walked back to his car, hand in hand, she'd never felt closer to another person.

Nor had she ever feared losing someone so much, because how in the world could she ever tell Boone she was an addict and had overdosed the same year his sister had? That she'd been clean for seven years, but the fear of relapse was never far away?

That evening at his party, the magnitude of Boone's parents' wealth continued to shock Julia. She recognized several of the people in attendance as political figures, and she'd swear one of the guests she'd seen talking with his brother earlier had a song on the current country music hits chart. Easily, there were a few hundred people inside the huge white event tent set up behind the home. White-cloth-covered tables with floral arrangements were surrounded by chairs, and there was a dance floor near a jazzy Memphis band playing.

Standing near the center of the tent, Boone greeted friends of his or of his parents one after another. Most of the evening, he'd had his hand on Julia's lower back, keeping her close. Even through her dress's fabric, his touch burned into her, making her wonder if he'd somehow short-circuited the logic centers in her brain. How could she be so aware of everything about him? Her nerve endings seemed to start right where his fingers began.

Earlier in the afternoon, when they'd gotten back to the estate and she'd been in the privacy of her room, she'd sobbed for his loss, for her own foibles, for how connected she felt to him when she knew his interest was fleeting. She showered and dressed in a bright blue dress she'd bought at her favorite consignment shop because she thought the color matched Boone's eyes. She'd been right.

Despite how awkward she felt, she smiled to the point that her face hurt. If she could have chosen, she'd have spent his birthday with him in a more relaxed private setting, something like what they'd done on Valentine's or a simple gathering with his family.

"My mother likes you," Boone whispered for her ears only. "She told me earlier after you'd gone upstairs to change."

Wondering what had prompted his unexpected comment, she glanced up. Wearing dress slacks and a tailored button-down, he looked handsome enough to steal her breath. "She was just being polite."

Because Julia's inner strength wasn't that admirable.

"She'd tell me if she didn't like you," he assured her. Then his expression tightened. "I told her that we went to the cemetery. You were right. She and Dad had been there."

"That's good."

He nodded. "Apparently, this isn't their first time. I should have gone sooner."

She put her hand on his shoulder, empathizing with the ache in his voice.

"Listen to me being all serious when we're at a party. Sorry."

"No worries. I'm glad you went earlier." And she was glad he'd trusted her enough to take her with him. Knowing he wanted a subject change, she glanced around the extravagantly decorated tent with its A-list attendees. "This isn't what I envisioned when you said your parents were throwing you a birthday party. You have a lot of friends."

"To be fair, the guest list includes family business associates and some of dad's and Justin's hospital colleagues who I don't know or barely know."

Still looking at the partygoers, her gaze collided with Leslie's. "Your mother may claim to like me, but I don't think your brother's girlfriend feels the same."

Boone didn't even glance toward the woman, just shrugged. "I did mention that she had me picked out as her sister's next boyfriend."

"Who was in the running for Miss Arkansas a few years ago." Boone hadn't looked nearly as impressed as Julia had been at the tidbit shared during breakfast that morning. "You should at least talk to Jacqueline to see if there's any chemistry."

"Quit trying to throw me at other women."

Flustered, she took a sip from her water glass. Was that what she was doing? She didn't want him to be with someone else. But she couldn't fathom him wanting to be with her when someone so beautiful was interested in him. Whether or not the woman was beautiful on the inside remained to be seen, but on the outside, she was stunning and belonged in Boone's world. "You should at least give her a chance."

Boone frowned. "She doesn't have a chance."

"You can't know that."

"I felt nothing when I met her, when I shook her hand, or heard her laughter." He stared directly into Julia's eyes. "There's no one I'd rather have spent today with than you, Julia. Not any part of today."

Heat flooded her cheeks, and she averted her gaze and searched for words to tell him that she felt the same, that there was nowhere she'd rather have been than by his side. But another couple came over to wish Boone a happy birthday, and she pasted on a smile as he greeted one of his former classmates. As he'd done all evening, he introduced her and included her in the conversation as much as possible when she had no history with any of the guests.

His mother stepped up and placed her hand onto Julia's upper arm. "Julia, dear, can I steal you away to introduce you to my cousin Martha? She's yet to meet you. We're as close as sisters, so she simply must meet the woman in my son's life."

"We're just friends," she reminded her, but Boone's mom just smiled and linked her arm with Julia's. As at the hospital, they weren't fooling anyone. Certainly, not even Julia's heart.

Boone excused himself from his friends, but his mother shook her head. "Stay. Catch up. We girls will be just fine for a few minutes. I promise to return her to you soon."

Hoping she didn't spill the water she held, Julia walked with Boone's mother across the tent to greet a stunning woman who appeared to be in her mid to late sixties.

"Julia, this is my cousin Martha, and Boone's godmother. She's been wanting to meet you all evening. I promised I'd steal you away from my son long enough for her to have a quick chat."

Julia blinked at Boone's mother.

The woman took Julia's free hand. "I was just telling Amelia that I had to meet the woman who'd stolen Boone away from Olivia. Such a sweet girl and from such a good family. We were all so surprised when they ended things, but meeting you brings it all into focus. He's quite smitten. Good for you for landing such a prize as my godson."

Julia started to correct the woman, to say that she and Boone were just friends, as she'd done with his mother moments before, and tell her that Boone had broken up with Olivia weeks prior to asking Julia out, but doing so felt a moot point. She sincerely doubted she and the woman would ever cross paths again as Memphis was on the opposite side of the state and she didn't expect her relationship with Boone to last. She certainly had no plans to come back to Memphis. Everyone was polite enough but mostly, she suspected they wondered what he was doing with the likes of her, rather than the beautiful Jacqueline or even Olivia.

"Nice to meet you." Rather than say more, she took another sip of her water. She wanted to escape back to Boone as quickly as possible, but his mother had other ideas and dragged her from the cousin over to meet another couple, a congressman and his wife.

Julia felt more and more out of place. She realized it was her own fault. Boone's mother wasn't trying to hide her in a corner since she was taking the time to introduce her and was genuinely pleasant. The problem was that Julia just didn't belong. She and Boone would leave the following morning, heading back to Knoxville and reality.

She glanced around the room, searching for him, and feeling both a nervousness and a peace when her gaze landed on him. He was standing with his brother, Leslie, and Jacqueline, laughing at something one of them had said. All gorgeous, they appeared to be straight from a glamour magazine. Smiling up at Boone, Jacqueline touched his arm. Julia's throat tightened. He belonged with someone like the beautiful woman who came from the right family and had the right background.

"She's wasting her time."

Julia's gaze cut to Boone's mother.

"Martha was right when she said my son is smitten. You're a lucky woman. I've never seen him so infatuated."

"Not even with Olivia?" she couldn't resist asking, then was completely mortified that she had done so.

Amelia shook her head. "Olivia is a wonderful woman, but she didn't put a light in my son's eyes the way you do."

"I—thank you." Guilt hit. "I don't know what he's told you, but we're not a couple. We're…it's complicated, but we're not a couple. Not really."

Amelia laughed. "He mentioned that you insisted upon being just friends until after your graduation in May. Prior to meeting you, I had my concerns that you were playing my son. I'll always worry about my boys, but he told me about going to the cemetery earlier, and I see how you look at my Boone. You'd never intentionally hurt him."

How did she look at Boone? As if he was the most wonderful thing to ever come into her life? In so many ways he was. He was also the most dangerous and might end up being the most devastating.

"I wouldn't, but I'm not sure we fit as anything more than friends."

"Why is that? You seem to get along well."

"We…we're just so different. My background is nothing like this." She gestured to their elaborate surroundings.

"Don't be deceived into thinking things make a person less human or hurt less. My son's heart is just as easily broken as any other man's who is in love with a woman. Treasure his affection for the gift it is."

Julia's eyes widened at Amelia's mistaken insinuation. "He isn't in love with me. Truly, we're not even dating."

Boone's mother's blue gaze pierced Julia. "But you are in love with him?"

"I— No— I mean—" Julia's head swam. She questioned if the room had started spinning. "I'm not in love with Boone." She wasn't. She couldn't be. Falling in love with Boone Richards would be foolish.

Amelia smiled rather smugly.

Averting her gaze from the woman's, she sought Boone's. He still stood with his brother and the two women. She wasn't in love with him. The thundering in her chest was nothing more than anxiety that she was such a fish out of water.

Only, looking at him, recalling when they'd been standing by the Mississippi, how she'd held onto his hand while he grieved at his sister's grave, she couldn't convince herself that there wasn't truth to what Amelia said.

Perhaps sensing that they were discussing him, Boone glanced up, met her eyes, and smiled in a way that left no doubt Julia was who he wanted. But lust wasn't the same as being in love with her. Swallowing the lump in her throat, Julia smiled back. For a short while, she got to have his attention focused on her in this fairy tale alter-universe.

His gaze not leaving hers, Boone excused himself from his brother, Leslie, and Jacqueline and headed toward Julia.

"You've had Julia long enough, Mom." He slid his arm around Julia's waist, his touch possessive enough that she wondered just how much she'd revealed when their eyes had met.

"You're right. I've stolen your lovely friend

much too long and must see to my other guests."
She smiled warmly, then kissed Boone's cheek.
"Happy birthday, dear. May all your wishes
come true."

They watched her walk away and be envel-
oped in a hug by a bear of a man who Julia had
been introduced to earlier as another cousin of
Boone's father.

"You're lucky to have her." Of all the things
she'd witnessed, his mother's love and protectiveness was the thing she envied. She'd known
from the way he spoke about her that they were
close. Meeting the woman and seeing how at
ease he was with her made it even more apparent. She had no doubt that Amelia Richards was
a killer businesswoman, but with Boone she was
melted butter.

"I am." He glanced around the tent, merry
with partygoers. "Let's get out of here for a few
minutes. You want to walk in the garden?"

"Your definition of a garden and mine are two
different things, but I'd love to get some fresh air
and escape from the crowd for a few minutes,
too." She paused. "Although it's your party, so
maybe we shouldn't?"

"It's fine. No one is going to miss me if we
duck out for a few minutes."

Julia doubted that but didn't press the point because she would like a few minutes away from

the others. Once outside the tent, Boone took her hand, and she didn't pull away, but instead marveled at how his touch could hold such strength and yet simultaneously be so gentle.

They walked around the immaculate garden for a while, hand in hand, talking, Boone pointing out his favorite play places as a child and Julia trying to imagine having grown up there. Come summer, flowers and fragrances would delight the senses, but Boone was what filled the night air. His handsome image was stamped permanently into her mind. His spicy male scent teased her nostrils. The amusement in his voice. The warm strength of his hand holding hers.

She loved him. Oh, God, she loved Boone.

"Tell me what you're thinking?"

Averting her gaze in case he could see her thoughts, Julia swallowed. "I—I left your present in my room."

"I can stop by later to get it."

She shook her head. "I don't think that's a good idea. I wouldn't want your mother to get the wrong idea."

"She doesn't think I'm a saint."

"I'm pretty sure you're wrong about that."

"Maybe. She's biased since she made me." He chuckled. "As far as the present, you didn't need to get me anything."

"I agree. I saw that big table of gifts. That's

insane." She glanced toward him. "What will you do with all that stuff?"

"Obviously, you didn't look close. The gifts are items to be donated to a local shelter that my mom sits on the board for."

Surprised, Julia stopped walking and turned toward him. "Your birthday presents aren't presents for you?"

Shaking his head, he pretended to pout. "It's terrible, isn't it?"

Stunned, she stared at him. "Is that something you suggested or just something your mother did?"

"More often than not there's a reason beyond what's on the surface when it comes to the parties my mother throws. My birthday was a great excuse for her to do a fundraiser for the shelter."

"She used you?"

He shook his head. "It's not like that. She's just a wise woman who knows how to take advantage of opportunities to do good. You surely don't believe I'd want all those gifts?"

Still taking in that Amelia had used the party for good, Julia shrugged. "I guess that depends upon what they are. I mean, if there was a set of keys to that old Corvette you want, then…"

He laughed. "You might be right." Sighing, he glanced toward the tent, noisy with music. "As much as I'd rather stay out here with you, we should go back."

Still hand in hand, they walked back and had barely made it inside the tent when his brother gestured for Boone to join him.

"Here is the birthday boy now," his brother announced. "Come on. I'm about to make a toast in your honor."

Boone glanced toward her, but Julia shook her head. She didn't want to be in the limelight of his toast, so she stepped back as he joined his brother near the band.

His brother made a big speech, causing several to laugh, including Julia.

"Now, if we could convince him to move back to Memphis," Justin continued.

Boone chuckled, listening as Justin recounted a story from their childhood. Would Boone eventually return to his hometown? It wouldn't surprise her. He probably had a contract with the hospital, and as soon as it ended, he'd relocate.

A woman coughed, causing Julia's gaze to shift that way. Next to her, Amelia's cousin Martha coughed again in an obvious attempt to clear her throat. Julia stepped closer.

"Are you okay?" she whispered, not wanting to draw attention to them during Justin's birthday toast to Boone.

Martha held up her hand, as if saying Julia

should hold on a minute, but whatever she'd been trying to clear with her cough must have shifted to block the woman's airway completely, because her hands went to her neck.

"Martha?" The woman's eyes watered, and her face reddened. "Is there something lodged in your throat? Are you choking?"

Martha gave a panicked nod, appearing more and more distressed.

"I'm going to do the Heimlich." Instinct kicking in, Julia moved behind the woman, wrapped her arms around her, placed her hands into the proper position, and gave a quick thrust. Nothing happened, so she gave another.

Still clutching at her throat, Martha sputtered. At this point, several nearby guests had realized that something was happening and had turned to observe what Julia was doing.

Ignoring them, she gave another hard chest thrust. Whatever had been stuck in Martha's airway shot forward. The woman gasped for air and simultaneously burst into tears. Relief swamped Julia so intensely that she fought doing the same. Helping the woman to a chair, she had her sit and knelt in front of her.

"It's okay. Just take deep, calming breaths," she encouraged, clasping Martha's hand.

Amelia rushed to them. "What's going on?"

"Martha got choked, and this woman saved her life," someone in the crowd said.

Glancing up, Julia saw they were surrounded by people. Justin had finished his speech, and most of the guests had lifted their glasses in cheers. Within seconds, though, Boone pushed through the crowd, as did his brother. Kneeling next to Julia in front of Martha, he began checking her. As Boone and Justin were both doctors, Julia started to move out of their way, but Boone stopped her. Justin had pulled out his phone and was calling for emergency services.

"Stay," he told Julia. Then he said to Martha, "I'm going to ask some questions. It's okay to just shake your head yes or no if you don't feel like verbally answering yet. Can you do that?"

The sobbing woman nodded.

"Can you take a deep breath?"

Martha did so, taking several.

"Do you feel as if anything is still hung in your throat, possibly blocking your airway?"

She started to shake her head, then looked uncertain. "I don't know."

Boone placed his ear against her chest, listening over multiple areas of her lungs. "I think whatever it was cleared, but you need to be checked to make sure your throat is okay. Sometimes dislodging a foreign object can cause trauma. Justin has called for an ambulance."

Still visibly shaken, Martha nodded. "I was so scared. I thought I was going to die."

"But you didn't, and everything is going to be okay." Boone placed his hand over where Julia clasped Martha's. "Thanks to Julia, you're going to be fine."

CHAPTER NINE

ALTHOUGH JUSTIN TRIED to convince Boone to let him go instead, Boone insisted upon riding in the ambulance to the hospital with Martha, saying he had a lot more experience with intubating someone if Martha's throat swelled. As a pediatrician, Justin conceded.

After the ambulance pulled away with Martha and Boone, Julia expected the partygoers to say their good-nights, but they didn't. All expressed their empathy for Martha, their appreciation of Julia's quick action, but then seemed to go back to enjoying the party as if nothing had happened.

Amelia gave Julia the biggest hug, thanking her, but even she had stepped back into the role of the perfect hostess. Julia supposed that since Martha should be fine, sending the guests home didn't make sense. But having played a direct role in the woman's life-threatening dilemma, she felt exhausted. As an hour turned into two with Boone still not back, she longed to go to her room. Deciding that no one would miss her if she slipped off for a bathroom break and a few minutes to just decompress, she headed into the house and toward the stairs that would lead to that section of the home.

"Wait," a young woman she'd met earlier called, chasing after Julia, drink in hand and sparkly designer bag bouncing at her side.

Saddened that her mini-escape had been interrupted, Julia pasted on a smile. She'd been introduced to so many different people that she had to rack her brain to recall the blonde's name. Patricia Brewer. Her family ran a popular restaurant chain. She'd batted her eyelash extensions at Boone so many times Julia suspected he might suffer from windburn.

"That was so cool what you did earlier." The woman's words slurred slightly, indicating she'd had a lot more to drink since their earlier interactions. "I could never have done that."

"With proper training, you could," Julia promised, looking at the woman more closely. Her pupils were constricted. Alcohol usually dilated one's pupils. What else had the woman taken, and how much, so that it counteracted the alcohol on her breath? "You should sign up for a CPR class. They teach the Heimlich and other lifesaving techniques. You don't have to be in the medical field."

"Oh, I'd be too nervous." The woman sipped

from her drink, raising Julia's concern for her safety. Drinks had flowed freely at the party, but she'd not noticed anyone grossly over-imbibing. This woman was intoxicated from something beyond what was in her glass.

"Are you okay? Will anyone be driving you home?" She wasn't sure what measure had been taken to prevent anyone from driving home who shouldn't, but Julia suspected someone as detail-oriented as Boone's mother had something in place. "It's Patricia, right?"

The woman blinked, causing another windstorm with her long lashes. "I rode here with a friend and am fine."

Julia wasn't convinced. Since Patricia wasn't driving, she wasn't sure what more she could do other than keep an eye on her and maybe get her to drink some water to sober up a little. Regardless, the woman's droopy-eyed expression concerned her. "Mixing alcohol with other substances can be dangerous."

"Quit being a party pooper." Patricia waved off Julia's concerns, sloshing some of her drink onto the gleaming hardwood floor in the process. Julia glanced around, but short of using her dress hem, there wasn't anything to clean the spill.

"I was heading upstairs to freshen up," she told the young heiress, planning to excuse herself from the awkward situation. "I'll grab tissue to clean that on my way back down. Can I bring you a water?"

"Oh, girl, I could totally use a bathroom break, too. I know they have those bathroom trailers set up outside, but I'd much rather go in here, you know?" To Julia's surprise, the woman draped her arm over her shoulder as if they were the best of friends, then giggled. "I'm Patricia, by the way."

"Um…yes, we met earlier." Julia cut her gaze to the woman, who was an excellent reminder of yet another reason Julia appreciated her sobriety. Crazy to think this could have once been her, that she'd not cared about her behavior or whether she was in control of her actions, or even if she remembered them the following day.

"My family has been close with the Richards for a long time."

Julia wasn't sure about having the woman come to her guest room, but she would let her go to the bathroom and hopefully convince her to change over to water. Maybe after she'd returned the woman to the party and cleaned up the spilled drink, she could escape for that bit of a break.

When they reached her room, Julia sat on the bed and let the woman go first, then went herself. When she came out of the bathroom, the woman was closing the top to a pill bottle.

Sweat instantly coated Julia's skin. "What did you just take?"

Shrugging, Patricia dropped the bottle into her purse and pulled out a cigarette package, tapped a cigarette free, then stuck it unlit into her mouth. "Just something prescribed. It's not a big deal."

Cringing at the thought of the woman possibly lighting the cigarette where the fumes would be trapped into her guest room, Julia equally wanted to make sure the woman was okay and to get her out of her room. She suspected the Richards didn't allow smoking in the house, and she sure didn't want her room to have the lingering scent. "I don't know you, but I do know how dangerous mixing medications with alcohol can be."

"I'm fine." She eyed Julia from where she sat on the bed. "Lighten up and let a girl have a good time. Just because Amy overdosed doesn't mean it's going to happen to the rest of us."

Julia winced at the woman's crassness. Had she herself really ever been like this?

"I work in an ICU where we see way too many overdose victims. Many of the overdoses were accidental. Please understand that I worry when I see someone putting herself at risk." Julia swallowed as memories flooded her. Memories of so many mistakes she'd made. Memories that made her panicky inside. "I volunteer at a recovery home. I imagine there's similar places in Memphis where you could get help."

"You have me all wrong. I don't have a prob-

lem." Eyeing Julia, Patricia took a long drag off
her unlit cigarette, then slowly blew out as if the
cigarette truly had been burning. "Other than
these things. They're what I'm trying to quit.
Nasty habit, but just having it in my mouth helps,
you know?"

Nothing she said was going to get through to
the woman. "I hope you're right, that you truly
don't have a problem. Let's head back outdoors
to the party."

"You don't know what it's like." Patricia stood,
then walked past Julia to toss her cigarette into
the bathroom trash. "You just don't know.

"I know better than you think." Julia got her
purse from the dresser and pulled out a business
card with a number she knew by heart. "This is
a twenty-four-hour hotline where you can get
help. Maybe tonight is a one-off and you don't
normally mix alcohol and medications. But the
pill you just took wasn't your first one of the
night. If you aren't able to stop on your own, call,
get help, check yourself in somewhere," she im-
plored. "Don't risk your life."

The woman took the card, glanced at it, then
flicked it onto the floor. "Who are you to judge
me?"

"No one." Once upon a time, she'd have acted
the same way if someone had suggested she get
sober. No one had. Not until Julia had lain in an

ICU and a compassionate nurse had made all the difference in the world. Julia strove to pay that kindness forward through her job and her volunteer work but recognized there was nothing anyone could do until a person was ready to make a change.

Sadly, sometimes they never got that opportunity.

Tossing his keys to one of the valets his mother had hired to keep parking from becoming chaos on the lawn and to call for transport for any intoxicated guests, Boone headed into the house. Cutting through was the quickest way to get back to the tent. He knew Julia understood that he'd needed to go with Martha, but he shouldn't have left her for so long at a party where she essentially didn't know anyone. As soon as he'd been sure Martha was stable with her husband and daughters by her side, he'd excused himself.

He didn't find Julia in the tent, and realized no one had seen her for a while. He texted but got no answer, so he headed into the house to go to her room.

"Julia? It's me." He knocked on her bedroom door. Was she inside? He pulled out his phone to try calling again.

The door swung open. Looking as if she'd just

awakened, she blinked. "You're back. You should have called. I'd have come down."

"I tried. Everything okay?"

"I came up to decompress a few minutes and dozed off." She yawned, then gave a guilty smile and tucked a stray strand of hair behind her ear. "Sorry. I can't believe I fell asleep. How's Martha?"

"They admitted her for observation, but her imaging didn't reveal any tears or significant trauma."

True relief showed on her face. "That's wonderful."

"Thank you for acting so quickly. You saved her life."

Her cheeks pinkened. "If I hadn't, someone else would have."

"Don't discount your actions. You saved her, and for that I am grateful." Feeling a little awkward at standing in her bedroom doorway, he asked, "Ready to go back down, or do you want to call it a night?"

"Going back to the party is fine. Just let me check that I don't have mascara smudges and look like a raccoon." She turned, then glanced back at him with excitement shining in her eyes. "Oh! I should give you your birthday present while you're here."

Glad that he wasn't having to bid her an early good-night, he grinned. "I admit I'm curious."

"It's just a little something that I thought would make you smile." Her own smile faded to a more hesitant expression. "But if you want to hurry back to the party, I can give it to you in the morning."

"I'm looking forward to opening your gift, Julia." Boone was in no rush to get back to the party. Everything that required his presence had ended long ago. He suspected the whole shebang would wind down within an hour as his mother would shut things down at midnight.

"You may be disappointed." She walked over to her bag and pulled out a small box. Her smile back, she held out the gift. "Happy birthday, Boone."

Having her here with him was the best gift. Boone opened the package. Inside was a toy version of his dream car. It was even the right color. He laughed. "This is great. Where did you find it?"

She looked pleased that he liked his gift. "Online."

He removed the car from the packaging, then spun one of the tiny wheels. "It's perfect." Just as she was. How fortunate was he to have met someone as kind, thoughtful, compassionate, talented, and smart as she was? Not to mention beautiful. Because with her smile brightening her face, no one could convince him that a more beautiful woman had ever lived.

"I'm not sure about perfect, but as close as my budget allows for." Happiness glittered in her eyes. He took her hand, giving it a gentle squeeze. "Thank you, Julia. For everything, especially for coming home with me this weekend and all the ways you've made this weekend special. I appreciate you going to the cemetery with me more than I know how to express. Other than what happened with Martha, it's been a wonderful birthday."

"You're welcome. Thank you for inviting me." To his complete shock, she stretched up on tiptoe and pressed a soft kiss to his cheek. When she pulled back, her cheeks pink, her gaze met his. "Happy birthday, Boone."

Explosions of color swirled through him, heating his insides until he wanted to burst from the intensity of her innocent kiss. There was little innocent about the way he wanted to pull her flush to him and kiss her until they were both breathless. Yet there was something so precious about the gesture that went way beyond the physical attraction he felt for her. He didn't know how to label those feelings, just that he'd never felt that way about anyone, and he longed to delve into exploring what was happening between them.

She'd graduate in May. He just had to be patient a little while longer. He just had to— His gaze landed on an oblong white tablet on the floor just at the edge of the bed.

Mind racing, he picked up the pill. Who had last stayed in the room, and how had the cleaners missed the tablet? His stomach knotted. What if someone with a child had been given the room? Julia looked at what he held, and he started to apologize that the cleaners had missed something that could have been treacherous if his parents had guests with a small child stay in the room. The guilt he saw on her face had sweat covering his skin.

He'd seen that look before on Amy's face.

Boone thought the pill was hers! Throat tightening, palms clammy, heart pounding, Julia shook her head in denial before he gave voice to what was clear on his face. "That's not mine. A woman was in my room earlier. Patricia Brewer. She wanted to use the bathroom. She must have dropped it while she was here."

Expression tight, Boone's jaw shifted. "There's bathrooms set up outside for guests. There was no reason for anyone to come to your room."

"Yes, I know, but—"

"Is that why you were asleep? Because you were doing drugs with Patricia? How could you do that, knowing what hell I went through with Amy's overdose?"

Julia took a step back. "I didn't do drugs with her, Boone. She had been drinking, but her eyes were constricted. I knew she'd taken something that had counteracted the effect of the alcohol, and I was concerned about her safety. She must have dropped the pill while I was in the bathroom."

Her words finally seemed to sink in.

"I'm sorry. I'm overreacting, aren't I? Going to Amy's grave today got to me more than I realized." He appeared gutted. "It caught me off guard to spot that pill on your floor, and then you looked— I don't know why my parents allow Patricia anywhere near this place. Mom believes she's recovered, but obviously she's not. Sometimes I think no one truly recovers from addiction." Boone raked his fingers through his hair. "You would never do drugs. I know that."

Did he really believe recovery wasn't possible? Julia's knees wobbled, and she sank onto the edge of the bed. Taking a deep breath, she knew what she had to do. What might destroy her world, but she had no choice. Not telling him beyond this moment would be unforgivable.

"About that... The truth is, Boone, that I would do drugs." Nausea rose up her throat as she forced herself to continue. "I would and I have."

Boone's face paled. "What are you saying?"

"I'm an addict."

"What do you mean, you're an addict?" Disbelief showed on his face along with a whole myriad of emotions that cut her to the quick. "You lied to me? You said this wasn't yours. Are you using drugs in my parents' home?"

"No. Sorry. I didn't word that well." Grateful she was sitting, she shook her head. "My thoughts aren't together. I hadn't planned to have this conversation tonight."

"You're an addict?" he repeated, his voice incredulous. "Telling me that is what you hadn't planned to do tonight? I'm so confused. What's going on, Julia? Are you trying to sabotage us again? Is that what this is?"

Embarrassed, and fighting devastation at the disillusionment she saw in his eyes, she lifted her shoulders. "I'm an addict, one who is seven years in recovery, but I don't fool myself that I'm not just one slipup from losing control. It's a battle I fight every day, and imagine I will for the rest of my life."

Boone grimaced as he held up the pill. "This isn't yours, but you'd have taken it if I hadn't found it?"

Would she have? She eyed the tablet in his hand. She knew exactly what it was and what milligram. She knew the way it would make her feel, the rush, knew the agony as it cleared from her system and her body craved more. She knew the risks.

"At one time, I would have. Pain medications were my drug of choice." Not for any physical pain she'd had, although she certainly hurt when coming off her high. Her pain had run much deeper than her body, to her very core. "But I took whatever I could get my hands on. I wasn't picky on how I numbed myself to the world."

Boone shook his head as if to dislodge her words. "I can't believe you're saying these things. You work in the ICU. You know what drugs can do to a person."

Knowing she had to tell him everything, she pressed on, wondering if the disgust would ever dim from his beautiful blue eyes, if he could ever look at her and see anything beyond her past. "I overdosed at twenty years old, Boone. I was in the hospital for weeks, then lived at a recovery house for several years, even after starting school. I've worked hard to stay clean since that time, sticking to the rules I wrote for myself to have a successful life."

"Yet you have a pill in your room."

"A pill that I told you wasn't mine." She tried not to flinch at the distrust in his expression. His face morphed into Clay's, and she heard the hateful words he'd once said to her, that he'd never be willing to tie himself to someone like her. Hadn't she always known Boone would feel the same? How foolish she'd been to let herself get caught up in his attention, to deep down want to believe that maybe, just maybe, Boone was different, that he could love all the parts of her, past, present, and future. She never should have allowed any of this to happen. The pain ripping through her chest was her own fault.

"It's not that I don't believe you. It's just—" Rather than finish whatever he was going to say, he paused, closed his eyes, and looked completely tortured. When he opened his eyes, sadness darkened them. "You know what happened with Amy, that she said she was clean, but then overdosed. You saw me today, how wrecked I am inside at losing her." His voice broke. "You should have told me months ago."

She should have told him. Yet her defenses were in full force and refused to lower. She'd worked hard to be a better person, and for what? To still never be good enough?

"I don't owe you a detailed history of my past, Boone. From the beginning, I told you that I didn't date, that you should move on to someone more suited. I never pursued you."

"So, I only have myself to blame for thinking you were different?"

She fought flinching. "If by different you

mean perfect and without flaws, then yes, you should blame yourself."

He did flinch, which pierced deep into her resolve. She could take no more. She just wanted to be home, to snuggle with Honey, and cry until there were no more tears to be shed.

Boone paced across the room, turning to look at her with red-rimmed eyes that continued the beating upon her heart. She'd caused this. Why had she ever thought that she might deserve happiness after the bad things she'd done?

"Stephanie mentioned your past a few times," he mumbled, perhaps to himself as much as to her. "I thought she meant your less than ideal childhood. I never dreamed she meant something like this."

Something like this. As if she were sullied and could never be good enough no matter how long she stayed clean. Clay had thought so. Apparently, Boone did, too. Maybe they were right.

She couldn't breathe. "Blame me. It's all my fault. I'm the one with the tainted past who is so far from perfect." She very seriously doubted he'd ever made such poor choices that he'd been homeless or so drugged out that he couldn't remember chunks of time. She knew better than to have let him behind her defenses. She'd subconsciously dared to dream when she should have strictly stuck to her rules. If she had, she'd be safe at home and not feeling as if her heart had been shredded. Fighting to keep from bursting into tears, she shrugged. "What does it matter at this point?"

"Because we'd never work anyway?" Hurt shone in his eyes.

"I've always known we wouldn't," she reminded him. "Now you understand. I'm sorry I didn't tell you everything sooner."

"You never gave us a chance, did you, Julia?" His expression tight, he walked over to the door, opened it, then paused. "You deceived me by omission and then crushed me with the truth. That's a lot for a man to take in. We'll talk tomorrow, but not until we've left here. I don't want my family hurt by this. Good night, Julia."

He closed the door behind him with a resounding click that echoed through Julia's heart.

If it was her heart breaking, why was it her eyes that leaked?

CHAPTER TEN

"WHERE DO YOU get off on leaving the way you did? Do you have any idea how upset I was when I realized you'd just left? How did you manage that, anyway?"

The following Monday morning, Julia glanced down the hospital hallway at several of her co-workers looking toward her, and she winced. She'd known she would eventually come face-to-face with Boone, that there was no avoiding it short of quitting her job—which she'd considered but decided against. She had run from her problems, her past, long enough. She'd known he'd be upset that she'd left, but no matter how many times she'd played the scenario over in her mind, she hadn't been prepared for the reality.

"I called for a hired car." She took a deep breath, then looked him directly in the eyes. Any affection he'd held for her was long gone, and only anger shone in the blue depths. Fine. Let him be angry. She was angry, too. Angry that he'd turned out to be no different from Clay, that he'd made her believe he cared for her. He'd only been caught up in the shiny package and not the depths of who she was.

"You taxied from Memphis to Knoxville?" he asked incredulously.

As many tears as she'd cried, she could have floated home.

"I taxied to a bus station and took a bus home, then called for another hired car to drive me from the station to my apartment." The drive had taken about nine hours to complete thanks to several stops along the way, but it felt as if it had been a hundred hours. But on that ride, she'd realized a lot of things about herself, who she was now, and who she was no longer going to be. Yes, she had a past. Who didn't? But she wasn't that person anymore. Rather than be ashamed of who she'd been, she was proud of the woman she'd become. If Boone, or any other man, couldn't see beyond her past, then they didn't deserve the woman she was today. "We're at work. This isn't the place to have this conversation."

"You should have thought of that when you repeatedly ignored my phone calls and text messages yesterday other than to message once to say that you were fine." His jaw worked back and forth, and then he blew out an exasperated breath. "*Fine*. Does anyone ever mean it when they use that word?"

He was right. She had set herself up for him to confront her at work. Although, truthfully, she'd thought he'd pretend she didn't exist rather than causing a scene. His ego must have taken a huge blow because she'd left Memphis on her own.

"I can't speak for others, but I am fine, Boone." If she knew nothing else about herself, it was that she was a survivor, and she would survive having fallen for him, too. She didn't need to check off all the items in a life success rule book to know she was a success. She got up every day and tried to make a difference in the world. Too bad if he couldn't see that. Maybe she even understood why he couldn't because of what had happened with Amy. Either way, she wouldn't let him or anyone else make her feel subpar ever again. She'd made mistakes, and she'd learned from them and become a better person. "If you'll excuse me, I need to check on my patient."

He rammed his hands into his scrub pockets, almost as if he had to do so to keep from reaching out. "That's it? You're just walking away from me?"

"Don't pretend that it's not what you were going to do to me."

His gaze narrowed. "I wouldn't have left you in Memphis."

"No, I didn't think you would, but I didn't want to be trapped in a car with you for six hours, either, when we both knew whatever this was between us was over."

He glanced toward their coworkers, then quickly looked away and pretended they weren't glued to what was happening. His gaze once again meeting hers, he stared at her for a long moment, then sighed. "Okay, have it your way. This isn't how I would have chosen things to be, but I could never put my family through the uncertainty of whether you'd relapse, anyway, so maybe it's for the best."

His words were echoes from Clay's lips and drove ice picks into her chest, piercing her heart. Surely it must be bleeding profusely. So much for her earlier bravado. No matter. As in the past, she'd rise out of the ashes. She rubbed her thumb across the tattoo on her wrist, then reached into her pocket to pull out a jeweler's box.

Barely able to continue to meet his eyes full of disillusionment, she called upon all her strength. "Lucky for you that you don't have to worry about that."

With her softly spoken words, she put the box into his hand, then walked away, head held high, and heart shattered.

Frustrated and watching Julia disappear into a patient's room, Boone closed his fingers around the jewelry box, knowing the diamond phoenix pendant was inside. How could she be so blasé about the fact that she'd left Memphis in the middle of the night without telling him? Her succinct text saying she was fine but wouldn't be riding back to Knoxville with him had completely gutted him.

He'd barely slept, thinking over the things he'd say to her while they drove back to Knoxville. He could make her understand why a relationship between them was impossible. After Amy's overdose, how could he risk that happening again? Instead, Julia had been gone, stunning him and his family, and he'd had six hours to stew.

Maybe she was right. Maybe it didn't matter, and at this point, the less said the better.

He slipped the jeweler's box into his pocket. He'd not wanted the pendant back. How could he when the phoenix belonged around her lovely neck? Had she taken great delight in shredding the calendar with his penciled-in dates?

"What did you just do?" Stephanie's question from behind him cut into his thoughts.

"It's not what I did that's the problem, is it?" Boone turned to meet Stephanie's accusing glare. "Rather than just saying that Julia had had a rough past, you could have gone into a little more detail and saved us both a lot of heartache."

"Really? That's what you think?" Stephanie's jaw dropped, and then her gaze narrowed. "If you can't see her for the beautiful person she is inside and out, then you don't deserve her."

Boone winced. "You don't understand."

He'd meant that they wouldn't have been in the situation that had happened Saturday night, that he'd have had all the facts. Then again, maybe if he'd told Stephanie about Amy, she would have revealed Julia's past. Or maybe she'd sensed there was a deeper problem, and that's why she hadn't told him.

"There is nothing you can say that will justify you hurting Julia," Stephanie spat at him. "Nothing. She's a better person than the both of us." Looking as if she'd like to say a lot more, scream a lot more, she took a deep breath instead. "To think I encouraged her to embrace what was happening with you because I thought you truly cared for her. Thanks for being as big a jerk as Clay."

"Who's Clay?"

"You'd have to ask Julia that, but I doubt she'd tell you, because you and he seem to have a thing for ripping the wings off of butterflies."

Was that how Stephanie saw him? How Julia saw him? As someone who had crushed a fragile being's spirit? Stephanie might see Julia as fragile, but her strength was one of the things Boone admired most. Still, what had this Clay done to her, and why did he want to punch the guy in the face for whatever it had been?

"How am I the bad guy here?" He'd been down this road with Amy. Knew how long someone could hide a problem until it was too late. How could he ever trust that Julia wouldn't relapse? His family had been devastated when Amy died. He couldn't risk putting them through that. Or maybe it was himself who he couldn't put through that again. "Julia didn't tell me the truth. Lying by omission is still lying. I'm not wrong to try to protect my family."

"Protect them from Julia?" Scoffing, Stephanie gave him an *are you crazy?* look. "Yeah, great job. She made herself vulnerable to you, and you stabbed her straight through the heart. You should be so proud."

"She's the one who walked away." His anger battled with so many other emotions. "She kept secrets, big secrets, and then she just left. Bash me if you want, but if anyone got crushed here, it's me."

Stephanie stared at him a moment. "Are you trying to convince me of that? Or yourself?"

Good question, and one that haunted Boone long after Stephanie had spun on her heel and walked away.

"Riley Sim," the dean announced over the loudspeaker at the University of Tennessee graduate school commencement ceremony the first Saturday in May.

Knowing she was next, Julia's knees shook. She didn't know how she was still upright. Her legs felt like jelly. Yet her head was held high. She'd done it. She'd turned her life around, gotten her bachelor's in science in nursing, held a respectable job she loved while attending graduate school to earn her master's degree, volunteered at a recovery home, and made a difference in the world. Check. Check. Check. Her Rules for Life Success book was full of check marks.

"Julia Lea Simmons."

An air horn blared from the audience section where a bunch of loud whoops and cries of "Julia!" sounded. Smiling at her friends' support, Julia crossed the stage, shook the dean's hand, accepted her diploma, and exited on the opposite side to make her way back to her seat. Inside, she was happy dancing. On the outside her smile had to be blinding people all the way to the top row of bleachers.

Hands trembling, she clutched the emblem of her hard work. Pride filled her.

After the ceremony, Stephanie, Derek, and the others who'd come to celebrate with her made their way through the crowded area where graduates, friends, and family were gathering for congratulations and photos.

Spotting them, warmth spread through her chest. She might not have blood family at the ceremony, but her tribe was there. Her people. She loved them and they loved her, even knowing all about her past and many flaws.

Swiping at happy tears, Julia nodded. "I'm so glad y'all came."

"Of course we came. I am so proud of you!" Stephanie squealed, wrapping her arms around her in a big hug as they jumped around together.

"We all are," Becky added as she and Dawn joined in on the hug and happy wiggling.

"Okay, guys, let's get in on this group hug," Cliff teased, spreading his arms around them, and causing them all to laugh as they pulled apart. "Seriously, Julia, you amaze me."

"Yeah, the only negative is that you've turned in your notice at the hospital." Stephanie poked her lip out in a big pout. "I am going to miss you so much."

There was that. Julia would miss the ICU crew terribly, too, but that a position had opened at the Knoxville House of Hope right as she'd graduated had been fortuitous. She'd considered staying at the hospital on an "as-needed" basis, working a couple of shifts per month, but ultimately, she'd decided that would only prolong the torture of being near Boone.

Boone. Oh, how her heart ached at his absence from her life the past month.

Part of her had hoped he'd be at her ceremony

and hear her valedictorian speech about rising from one's ashes and achieving anything one set their mind to, no matter their past. That he'd choose to be there along with their friends, celebrating this huge milestone. But his wasn't one of the smiling faces congratulating her. When they'd had to interact at the hospital, he'd been cordial, professional, but he'd been little more than that for weeks. For the most part, he'd avoided her and vice versa. No way would he have come today and risk giving her false illusions that he had any interest in her.

That was all right. She was okay and would continue to be okay. She didn't need Boone to have a happy life. She was happy. Mostly. Now she'd be able to make an even bigger difference in the hope that others would be able to overcome their addiction and achieve recovery, too. She'd serve as an example. If she could do it, anyone could.

Determined she was going to focus on the day's many positives despite the hole in her heart that only Boone could fill, she smiled, posed for photos, and embraced her friends and the love they showered on her. No matter what, she would soar.

"Um… Julia?"

Julia didn't need to turn to see what Stephanie was looking at. Who she was looking at. Julia's insides had gone into full Boone-is-near mode. Why was he there? Swallowing, she spun toward where her friend was staring.

There, holding the world's largest bouquet of red roses, stood Boone.

Boone had stood back, allowing Julia to enjoy her moment with their friends prior to making his presence known. He'd not sat with them, but they'd known he was there, known that he couldn't miss one of the most important days of Julia's life.

Wearing her cap and gown and the happiness that came with success, she'd never looked more beautiful. "Congratulations, Julia."

"Thank you." Her brown eyes studied him. "I wasn't expecting you to be here." Her gaze moved past him to the people he'd sat with during the ceremony. "Any of you." Confusion clouded her face. "But I don't understand why you're here."

"I couldn't keep them away," Boone began, thinking perhaps his family should have stayed in the background. "But they have orders to not say a word until I've gotten out the words I've spent the past four weeks trying to perfect."

He moved closer to her and handed her the flowers. "These are for you."

She glanced down at them, then back up at him. "Thank you. They're lovely."

"This is also for you." He reached into his pocket and pulled out the jeweler's box that held her pendant.

"I can't take that back."

"It belongs to you, Julia. It has from the moment I saw it. You are a bright and burning flame that lights up the world for all those lucky enough to be in your presence." He opened the box and removed the necklace. "Allow me?"

Looking hesitant, she finally nodded. He moved behind her and slipped the chain around her neck, then closed the clasp. "There," he said, coming face-to-face with her again. "It's back where it belongs."

"Thank you. I admit, I'd gotten used to wearing it as I hadn't taken it off until that night in Memphis." Her cheeks flushed from her memories. "I shouldn't have left like I did."

"I didn't deserve for you to stay," he admitted. Then, glancing around at all their friends and his family hanging upon his every word, he said what they'd come to hear. "I messed up, Julia. I could go into all the reasons I did so, but none of them stand up to the reality that I lost you in the process. Nothing is worth not having you in my life."

Her throat worked, catching his eye, and he continued. "You once agreed to allow me to take you out to celebrate your graduation. I'd like to hold you to that."

She blinked. "You want to take me to dinner? That's what this is? A date?" She grimaced. "Don't think me ungrateful for the flowers and for having my necklace back, but I've already been with a man who didn't see my worth, Boone. From the point I told him about my past, that's all he could see when he looked at me. I'm much more than that and won't live being treated that way. I deserve better."

"I don't see your past when I look at you, Julia." He took a deep breath and hoped his next words conveyed all the things in his heart. "It's my future I see."

"I don't understand."

"I'm in love with you, Julia. I think I have been from the moment you stripped me of my bear blanket." He smiled at the memory. "I don't deserve forgiveness for what happened in Memphis, but I'll spend the rest of my life making up for it if you'll give me the chance."

Stephanie and the girls let out a collective *aww*. Boone's mother clasped her hands together and the guys all stared at Julia, waiting for her response, but none so intently as Boone.

"You're in love with me?"

"I figured the roses would give me away."

"Because they're red?"

"They stand for love."

Glancing down at the flowers, she closed her eyes. When she opened them, she nodded. "You're right, they do." The moment the words were out of her mouth, she shoved the flowers back into his hands. "Here."

She'd given back his flowers. She didn't want his love. He'd blown any chance he had of winning her heart because of how he'd handled her sharing her darkest secret with him.

He shook his head. "No, I won't take them back, Julia. They're yours."

Her gaze met his, and what he saw had his breath catching. "Red roses are for love, Boone."

"You love me?"

"With all my heart."

Around them, their friends and family clapped and whistled, but Boone focused only on Julia. "I love you, Julia."

He pulled her to him and, handing her roses to an about to burst Stephanie, Julia willingly went, cupping his face between her hands. "No more secrets, Boone. I promise to always be honest with you, even when the truth may not be so easy to share."

"And I promise to always support you, Julia. In your career, in your school, in your sobriety, and in your moments of weakness. I'll be there to keep your fire burning so you can continue to shine."

And he did.

EPILOGUE

WITH HER BEAR blanket wrapped around her, Julia shook the Christmas package Boone had just handed her. The box was of a similar size as the previous year's gift, and the rattle inside was suspicious.

She glanced up at him and guessed, "Did you get me another calendar? I've really enjoyed checking off our dates on last year's."

"You'll have to open it to see."

"But Christmas isn't for two more days."

"True, but we leave for my parents' tomorrow morning, and I wanted to give you this before we go."

"I don't mind waiting until we're there. It'll give me something to open that morning."

"You think my mother isn't going to lavish you with gifts? According to Justin, half the gifts beneath my parents' tree have your name on them. He's even lodged his complaint that Honey has more gifts than the rest of us."

"Your mother and my cat have definitely bonded," Julia mused, smiling as she shook the box again. "Okay, if you're sure you want me to open it early, then I will."

"Glad I could twist your arm that way," he teased.

"Hey, I'm not opposed to waiting," she shot back.

Taking his phone out to snap photos while she opened her gift, he motioned for her to proceed. Julia tore into the paper, laughing when, saving the smaller box for last, she pulled out a calendar for the upcoming year. Rather than corny doctor jokes, this one had corny nurse jokes.

Opening it to the first the page, she read, "'Ski with Boone at Friends-mas.'" On January first.

Flipping the page, she laughed when she read, "'Break Val-friend-tine tradition by making out with Boone.'"

In March, he'd written, "Go green with Boone" on the seventeenth and "Give Boone birthday kiss" at the end of March.

But when she read April's message, she glanced up to see he'd propped his phone so it recorded her hands-free, and he'd moved next to the sofa.

"'April showers…'" She turned to the following month. "'…bring May…'" She looked at him in question. "Did you forget to write *flowers*?

Because that's what April showers bring. And if you didn't pencil in any dates for us in April or May, should I be worried?"

Grinning, he knelt next to her and gestured to the smaller package that had been inside the larger box along with the calendar. "You better open your other package before you look at the rest of your year."

Curious, she reached for the smaller package that was of similar size to the previous year's jeweler's box. "Did you get me earrings to go with my necklace?"

The necklace she'd not taken off since he'd put it around her neck on her graduation day.

"Open and see."

She opened the lid and gasped. "Boone?"

His eyes full of everything she could possibly have hoped for, he gestured to her calendar. "Turn the page, Julia."

"My hands may be too shaky," she warned, not quite believing what was happening. She'd known Boone loved her. He showed it to her every day in all he did, but she hadn't dared to let herself dream of what was happening. Or at least, what she thought was happening. Holding her breath, she exchanged May for June. Her vision blurred with tears, but she read, "'Julia marries Boone.'" On the following day, he'd written, "'Julia and Boone live happily ever after.'" And he'd drawn a line indicating it included the rest of the month, then the following, and so on through the end of the calendar.

"I…um…think you're going to have to return this," she managed, staring up into the most beautiful blue eyes she'd ever seen. "Someone's scribbled in it."

"You know how doctors' handwriting can be," he quipped, as he'd done the previous year, then knelt beside her and took her hand. "Will you, Julia?"

"You're sure that's what you want?"

"I'm sure you're what I want, who I want, now and forever. I want the world to know you're mine."

"Hmm, and all this time, I thought it was the other way around, that you were mine," she teased.

Lifting her hand to his lips, he kissed it, then took the ring from the jeweler's box. "Marry me, Julia. Pick whatever day you want. Just pencil me in for every day for the rest of your life."

"Yes." Tears of joy ran down her face. "You know my answer is yes. I adore you and can't imagine life without you."

"Then don't ever," he ordered, sliding the diamond ring onto the fourth finger of her left hand. "Just put me at the top of every page of your Rules for Life Success."

"The way you've put yourself on every page of my calendar?"

His gaze met hers, and he gave her a sheepish grin. "You have to admit it worked out pretty well for me this past year."

"For both of us." She stared at the ring. "I promised to always be honest with you, though, so I have to tell you that I tossed my rule book. I don't need to check items off a list to know I have a successful life, not anymore. As long as I'm clean, helping others, and you keep penciling yourself into my calendar, I know I'm doing something right, and that's all the affirmation I need."

He laced his fingers with hers. "Just wait until you see what I have in mind for next year. Good thing I have a year to figure out if I want to use blue or pink ink."

Filled with a giddiness that surpassed any high she'd ever known, Julia wrapped her arms around his neck. "Why not both? After all, you're a twin, so it's possible."

Not only possible, but Julia and Boone's reality, nine months after they said, "I do." A boy and a girl and their very own happy-ever-after.

* * * * *

*If you enjoyed this story, check out
these other great reads from
Janice Lynn*

Heart Doctor's Summer Reunion
The Single Mom He Can't Resist
Reunited with the Heart Surgeon
Weekend Fling with the Surgeon

All available now!